"This Is A No-strings Offer."

David felt the need to make the statement, even when the heat between them continued to flare. "We're going to land, have a quick lunch on the way to the gallery and then look at some artwork before supper. If after supper you want to go straight to your room alone, that's your call."

He meant it. No matter how much he wanted to be with Starr, it would be mutual or not at all. "We have enough history between us for you to know that I would never hold you to something unless you want the same thing."

She stared back into his eyes, holding on for a long drone of the private jet's engines before finally nodding. "I trust you."

"Good. Good."

He was glad she did, because staying strong against the temptation of sleeping in the room next to Starr would be total torture. He wasn't so sure he'd just made the wisest move.

Dear Reader,

If you've read the book prior in my Beachcomber series, you know that my current Silhouette Desire story features a heroine under foster care who grew up in a Southern antebellum home—a subject dear to my heart. When my husband and I married, we planned on a large family and promptly had four children. We had long discussed the option of a foster child or overseas adoption, when lo and behold, our next very special child found his way to us during the string of hurricane disasters that struck the Gulf Coast in 2004. Now our newest but oldest son has joined our fold, and what a constant blessing and joy he is!

I would like to encourage those of you who also feel called to expand your family to consider programs such as the foster care system, adoption, overseas adoption, Big Brother/Little Brother, Big Sister/Little Sister. There's a wealth of children out there waiting to be hugged and loved!

Also, I hope you will check out my next HQN release, *On Target,* July 07, when my flyboys take to the skies for their hottest mission yet!

Thanks again for all your letters. I do so enjoy hearing from readers! If you would like to contact me, I can be reached at Catherine Mann, P.O. Box 6065, Navarre, FL 32655 or www.CatherineMann.com.

Happy Reading!

Cathy Mann

UNDER THE MILLIONAIRE'S INFLUENCE

CATHERINE MANN

Published by Silhouette Books
America's Publisher of Contemporary Romance

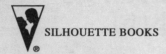 SILHOUETTE BOOKS

®

ISBN-13: 978-0-373-76787-8
ISBN-10:   0-373-76787-0

UNDER THE MILLIONAIRE'S INFLUENCE

Visit Silhouette Books at www.eHarlequin.com

Printed in U.S.A.

Recent Books by Catherine Mann

Silhouette Desire

Baby, I'm Yours #1721
*Under the Millionaire's
 Influence* #1787

Silhouette Intimate Moments

*Grayson's Surrender #1175
*Taking Cover #1187
*Under Siege #1198
*Private Maneuvers #1226
*Strategic Engagement #1257
*Joint Forces #1293
*Explosive Alliance #1346
*The Captive's Return #1388
*Awaken to Danger #1401
*Fully Engaged #1440

Silhouette Books

*Anything, Anywhere, Anytime

*Wingmen Warriors

CATHERINE MANN

RITA® Award winner Catherine Mann resides on a sunny Florida beach with her flyboy husband and their five children. Although after nine moves in eighteen years, she hasn't given away her winter gear! Since landing on the shelves in 2002, she has celebrated twenty releases, a slot on the Waldenbooks Bestseller's List and been a five-time RITA® Award-finalist. A former theater school director and university teacher, she graduated with a degree in theater from UNC-Greensboro. Catherine loves to hear from readers and chat on her message board—thanks to the wonders of wireless Internet. which allows her to cyber-network with her laptop by the water! To learn more about her work and her latest moving adventures, visit her Web site at www.CatherineMann.com.

To Jasen:
Our newest child, but also our oldest. We love you, son!

One

Starr Cimino vowed to invest in new pjs, even though her love life was currently on life support.

Facing her arch nemesis in a threadbare Beachcombers Restaurant T-shirt before she'd even had her morning coffee just sucked. So much for armor to gird her five-foot stature.

Her steely spine and some wit would have to suffice. She braced her back and stood down the strong and vital force filling the door of her seaside carriage house in Charleston, South Carolina.

She didn't doubt her ability to deck anyone who threatened her. She'd learned young to take control of her life after all her crook parents had forced her to endure. But it just wasn't cool to take out a seventy-eight-year-old lady in a housedress. The mother of the man to whom she'd given her heart and virginity.

At least she could reclaim her heart.

Swiping the sandy sleep from her eyes, Starr forced a smile taught to her by her foster mother, "Aunt" Libby. "What can I do for you, Mrs. Hamilton-Reis?"

Other than toss some blue food coloring into her fish pond so the old bat's prize guppies would look more like a certain current cartoon fish. Okay, so Aunt Libby's training hadn't totally saturated Starr's conscience as a teen.

Grudges. Man they hurt the soul and she really should get over it, but this lady had treated her worse than the scum on her fish pond for right around seventeen years.

And God forbid Starr should date the woman's precious heir.

So Starr and David had met behind sand dunes and shimmied up the rose terrace to climb into his bedroom window during their teenage romance that had swelled and broken her heart in one tumultuous year.

"What do I want?" Alice Hamilton-Reis's voice rose and fell along with the rush of the waves along the shore. "I want your relatives to move their RVs out of my neighbor's view."

Her family? Here?

Prickles spread over her as she looked around and found that, yes, there were three RVs parked right on the grass between the Hamilton-Reis's historical plantation house and Starr's carriage house. The same RVs she'd ridden in before luck and an efficient social worker had intervened.

Crap.

She shoved her hands through her snarled mess of hair, as if that might somehow restore order to her rapidly tangling world. No luck. In fact…the worst luck sauntered into view with broad shoulders and serious temptation.

David. Her attention skipped off those RVs pronto.

He took the lengthy porch steps of his family's Southern antebellum mansion with the same confident strides he'd possessed even as a lanky teenager who'd sent her pulse skyrocketing. David made clothes look good, no question. He wore formal dark pants with loose hipped ease, a crisp white shirt contrasting against his jet-black hair and a tan that attested to time spent in the sun.

Her heart rate still doubled, but for another reason. Yes. Because of their history and how he'd so deeply bruised her tender feelings over ten years ago with his all-or-nothing ultimatums. He wanted her to give over her hard won control of her life, and heaven help her, he'd once truly tempted her. And when she'd seen him again a year ago, her willpower had been in the negative numbers. They'd landed in bed together in seconds flat. Then they'd found their clothes again, he'd stuck to his same, unflinching party line—pick up and follow him around the world, leave behind the only home she'd ever known. His way.

Not a chance.

She didn't want to think overlong on the fact that she hadn't been with anyone since then—thus her crummy lingerie and love life gasping for breath. She would hold strong this time, regardless of her body already tingling to life again.

Lord knew she had enough to think about dealing with her biological parents showing up—*don't look, don't look, don't look at those RVs yet*—and David's perfect-lineage mama staring her down.

David stopped on the bottom step and yet still he stood around the same height as the women on the porch, darn him. "Mother, you shouldn't be outside in the morning damp air." A hand towel draped around his neck attested his recent shave, yet he still looked totally calm and collected even though he'd obviously rushed out after his mother. "Your doctor said for you to keep your feet up until the new blood pressure medicine takes effect."

Great. She *had* to be nice to the old bat or she ran the risk of David's mother stroking out on the carriage house stairs.

Aunt Libby's voice echoed through her head. Manners. Manners.

Jeez. She searched for something to say. Seagulls and cranes swooped for breakfast along the shore. Distant church bells from downtown Charleston chimed seven.

Starr tugged at the T-shirt and pretended she wore her favorite form-fitting jean dress and wedge heels with ties that wrapped around her ankles. She was good at the princess pretense. She'd perfected it as a gypsy child on the road. She refused to let herself be ashamed for things they had done—the things they'd insisted she do. She reminded herself she was a businesswoman now. She and her two foster sisters had turned Aunt Libby's mansion into Beachcombers—an up-and-coming restaurant.

She sidestepped cranky Alice and faced her old lover who looked too darn good for this early in the morning, his dark hair glistening with water from a recent shower. Saints save her from her vivid imagination. "Hello, David, your mother and I were just discussing a better parking place for my, uh…" She couldn't bring herself to use the word *family.*

They'd given up that right when they'd left her in the foster child system for years on end. Doing nothing to bring her home, yet doing nothing to cut her loose for adoption.

Mrs. Hamilton-Reis turned to cling to her son's arm as if suddenly weak. "We need to get those recreational vehicles situated elsewhere. Surely it would be better for her business if they were over there on the beach rather than in plain view of her restaurant."

Of course his mother always put a better spin on things when he was around…not that she could really think much about his dear old ma when he was moving closer by the second and saturating Starr's senses.

Now that he was closer, she could see the monogram on the hand towel draped around his neck. The tangy scent of his aftershave wafted up the steps to tease her senses along with the salty scent of the ocean breeze. All of which stole her self-control much like waves stole sand from the shore.

And darn him, the way his eyes heated over her, it didn't matter what she wore.

Starr turned to Mrs. Hamilton-Reis, a hefty reminder of why she needed to keep her distance from David. "I'll talk to them about parking closer to the beach where the lawn's already patchy."

David's mother surveyed the lawn. "That'll be much better for business, my dear." Alice patted her son's arm. "Thank you for worrying about me. I'll be having breakfast on the veranda with my feet up. It would be lovely if you could join me."

He nodded. "I'll be in shortly."

The woman who'd once never passed up an opportunity to tell Starr she shouldn't hold David back from pursuing his dreams pinched a smile as she started her pivot away. "I'm glad we could work this out, dear."

Starr scrunched her eyes closed with a sigh. Still the tequila sunrise bled through her lids to sparkle through her brain. Or was that all the emotion bubbling through her?

David. Her parents. Alice Hamilton-Reis. All at once. Too much.

She'd forgotten how the woman would speak nicely to her whenever David was actually around. Not that she'd ever been outright mean to Starr, just coolly disapproving until icicles formed in the spiral curls of Starr's hair.

She shook free the insecurities of her youth and opened her eyes. Yep, David was still here and dear old mom was gone. Time to deal. Fast. Before the RV crew woke up and she had her hands more than full of frustration…*and pain,* a little voice whispered.

No. She was an adult, a businesswoman who currently had a hunky, tempting piece of her past standing on her porch. "So, you're back from…wherever it is you traveled this time."

Even though his inheritance enabled him to sit back and never work if he chose, David still served as a civilian employee for the air force's OSI—Office of Special Investigations. He traveled the globe, slipping in and out of countries often undetected, just as he'd always planned during their teenage years, dreaming on a beach blanket under the stars. Even back then he'd wanted her to come along when the mission permitted and even then her root-seeking heart had quaked.

Taking the rest of the steps to join her, he stuffed his hands in his pockets and hitched one shoulder against her porch post, close. *So* close. "I was in Greece working on a NATO counterterrorism task force."

"Wow, you can actually share what you're doing. That's rare." How many times had she wondered? Too many for her comfort level. "It sounds really awesome."

He stayed modestly—or covertly—quiet. The distant sound of waves and the breakfast crowd heading into the restaurant next door faded away as she couldn't help but focus on him.

Her babbling mouth ran away from her. "I imagine this is one of those missions you always talked about me coming along with you."

David cocked a brow, his head tipping to the side even if he still stayed quiet. Embarrassment heated through her with a need to fill the silence. God, he could still undo her thoughts as easily as he'd once undone her bikini top.

"But we both know that's old ground. Like I really could have picked up and gone to Greece now anyhow. I have a business to run, obligations to my business partners, my sisters. Still it sounds really exotic."

Her foster sister Claire would have relished experiencing the exotic foods. They served mostly down-home Southern cuisine at Beachcombers, but Claire still enjoyed adding something a little different every now and again.

Once upon a dream, Starr had contemplated taking a trip or two to study the great artists of the world. Except, bottom line, she didn't want to spend her entire life on the road. She'd done enough of that for the first ten years of her life with her gypsy family.

Now, she thrived on the security of waking up to the same gorgeous ocean sunrise every morning. Her little carriage house behind Beachcombers might not be much, but it was hers. A home.

"Exotic?" he quipped. "Time was you thought that sounded too far from home."

Suddenly she couldn't hold onto the fantasy any

longer. No princess clothes or armor. Nothing but old pain and a worn out T-shirt. "Do we really want to walk down that road again today, David?"

He plucked at the shoulder of her shirt and pulled off a crumpled bit of a tissue-paper flower. Great. The fates must be plotting against her. Not only did she look like crap, but she also had arts-and-crafts bits and pieces stuck to her like a third grader.

David held up the silvery flower she'd been using to make personalized wrapping bags for wedding-shower party favor gifts for her restaurant. One corner of his mouth kicked into that confident smile that never failed to flip her stomach into somersaults to rival her circus gypsy cousins' talents. David tucked the crackly bloom behind her ear.

His knuckles skimmed her cheek in a touch so soft but undoubtedly deliberate. She knew him. Knew his touch well from their high-school romance.

And yes, from their brief time together a year ago when she'd been unable to resist him. Heaven help her, she couldn't spend the rest of her life jumping into bed—or against a wall—with David Reis every time he breezed through the United States.

Starr stepped back. "I'll keep my eyes open for your mother. Leave your cell-phone number and I'll call if I see her wearing herself out."

"Thank you."

She thought about asking for more details about his mother's health, even sympathizing since it was his mother after all, but then realized that would keep him on her porch longer. And when they spent any lengthy amount of time together, they ended up arguing and he ended up kissing her silent. She mentally kicked herself and mumbled, "God, we're both such idiots."

He cocked an arrogant brow. "What was that?"

"We both need to get to work." She backed up to grip her door. "I really need to get dressed, so…"

"Drag my sorry ass off your porch."

A laugh bubbled before she could squelch it. She so enjoyed his dry sense of humor. She couldn't resist it, either. "You said it, not me."

Starr slid away and sagged against the door inside her carriage house filled to the brim with her arts-and-crafts supplies. Victorian eclectic. *Hers.*

She exhaled long and hard.

She'd held strong, gotten her way. She was alone in her little house. She'd kept her distance from David. *And* she'd managed to shoo him away before her folks made their morning showing.

Thank you, Aunt Libby, for putting in a good word with the Man upstairs on that one.

But she couldn't count on Aunt Libby holding back the tide forever. With her luck, her family would set up Porta Pottis and charge folks for using them. Her ma and da never missed a chance to make a buck, and if they could land a dollar without working, all the better.

Ma and Da. Why she couldn't distance herself enough to call them Gita and Frederick instead, she didn't know. She wanted Aunt Libby, her foster mother, Mom.

All a moot point and waste of time to consider at the moment. Gather up those scattered thoughts before David had a chance to slip past her defenses.

But she couldn't understand why the fates had been so vengeful as to send those campers full of ex-family, who'd rejected her, used her, stolen from her, at the very same moment that David had chosen to make one of his rare appearances in Charleston.

Two

"The way you wield that hot glue gun, it's no wonder you sleep alone. Men must be hitting the floor in terror."

Claire's words rattled around in Starr's head with a little too much accuracy. Nothing like a sister—even the foster sort—to put you in your place. Starr spread her gift bags, glitter and shells along the kitchen butcher block as she put together the tissue paper. At least the RV crew had decided to sleep in today and give her a couple extra hours to gather her thoughts after seeing David had rocked her balance.

She simply wanted a half hour of peace to pull herself together. Tough to find with such a perfect contrasting view of the three rickety RVs and David's Lexus right there, reminding her of so many painful moments in her past.

But damn it, she would put a time stamp on that segment of her life because her days of romance with David had expired long ago.

She stared out the open window at the three parked vehicles. Her sister worked by her side decorating a cake, while two part-time help gals took care of the remaining breakfast crowd. The gentle ocean breeze ruffling the lace curtains may have cooled the steamy kitchen, but it did nothing to cool the steam curling inside her after a simple encounter with David.

She might well need more than a half hour.

Starr globbed another dollop of oozing glue on the magenta bag. "I imagine you've waited a whole year for that payback line just because I teased you about the way you whacked around a swizzle stick when you were mad at Vic."

Her sister had fought hard against falling in love, even contemplating single motherhood, until finally the burly veterinarian had won her over.

Earth-mother-type Claire swooped her cake-frosting spatula through the air. "Aha! So you *are* mad at a man."

Had she really just jumped into that net because she was busy thinking of her sister's tangled love life from last year? "Don't you have a baby to nurse?"

The multicolored sling around Claire's neck held the

infant snuggled securely to her chest. "Little Libby is snoozing away, happy and fully fed."

No surprise Claire managed yet another addition to her life with ease. Her unflappable, organized sister always had. Even her silky blond hair cooperated to make a smooth look along with the clean lines of her conservative clothes. Claire would never put together mismatched designer-fashion finds Starr liked to scoop up at the Salvation Army. But then Starr couldn't quite stifle the colors in her wardrobe any more than she could quiet her bright artwork.

Claire gently patted her baby girl's bottom. Motherhood suited her well. She'd obviously taken on all the traits of their foster mother.

Aunt Libby had been an eccentric—amazing—woman. Having lost her fiancé in the Korean War, she'd never married, instead devoting her life to taking in foster daughters. Countless foster girls had channeled through her antebellum home, money in short supply, love in abundance. Most had either returned to their homes or found new adoptive parents. All but three had left—herself, Claire and Ashley, who'd just graduated from college with her accounting degree. Her graduation being the reason for their flurry of preparations today, to put together a surprise party.

Their shy younger sister would work herself into a tizz if she had time to think of an impending celebration, so they'd opted for low-key festivities as a surprise party. Ashley deserved to have her accomplishments lauded. A whiz kid, she'd been keeping the Beachcombers' books since the doors had opened two years ago.

Starr brandished her hot glue gun, which of course made her think of all the times she'd seen David's gun tucked in a shoulder harness. So often she thought of the glamour of his world travel, but the danger sent a sliver of…*something,* something she didn't want to consider overlong because it traveled up her spine to sting her eyes. "Okay, so I'm armed and fearsome. Why does that have anything to do with a man?"

Claire brandished her own decorator gun, swirling Congratulations, Ashley across the cake festooned with pink roses. "It's the way you're wielding it, big hot globs that don't allow for anything to slip away."

So? "And that tells you what?"

"The same thing you've always wanted where David Reis is concerned." Claire set her frosting aside and pinned her sister with her ever-wise older gaze. "You want to glue his wandering feet to the ground."

"Or glue his arrogant mouth shut." Now that called for a huge blob.

Claire tapped Starr's toe with her flip-flop-shod foot. "But then he wouldn't be as fun to kiss."

Starr couldn't help but shiver in agreement at that. "You're a wicked woman."

"I'll plead the fifth." She winked as she topped off another cabbage rose on the cake. "How long is he in town this time?"

"I didn't ask." But yeah, she wanted to know. Not wise.

"You're kidding."

"His mother was there at first, and then my, uh—" she swallowed hard "—relatives could have stepped out at any second."

Claire's hand fell on her shoulder. Her sister always did try to mother the world. "Speaking of which, why are they here?"

"I honestly don't know." Starr eased out from under the comforting hand that could too easily make her go all emotional when she needed to hold herself together more than ever. She had genetics working against her when it came to being overly dramatic. It was one of the things that used to drive David nuts. "I haven't asked them yet, but I promise I'll get to it right away. I won't let them interfere with business."

"I'm not concerned about that, honey, I'm worried about you." She gripped Starr's shoulders again and turned her back around. "I don't want them to take advantage of you."

God, the truth still hurt because undoubtedly they wouldn't have shown up for any other reason. Bracing herself to hold on tight to her emotions, Starr wrapped her arms around her sister in an awkward hug, the snoozing baby between them.

Claire patted her back. "We're a team, sister. Don't ever forget it. You don't have to take them on alone. Say the word and I'll walk over with you."

Sniffling in spite of her best intentions, Starr leaned back and flicked her hair over her shoulder. "Thanks, but I'm a tough cookie in case you haven't noticed. I have my killer glue gun, after all." Bravado in place, she retrieved her gun and her resolve.

And darned if one of those RVs didn't start moving with the first signs of life from inside, shock absorbers obviously having long ago given up the ghost.

Ghosts.

She could talk about bravery and guns and time stamps all she wanted, but it would take a lot of stamping to eradicate all the ghosts clamoring around in her head.

David slid his arms through his suit jacket on his way out the front door. He needed to report in and sign leave papers to take the time off to make sure all was well with his mother's health.

And to figure out what the hell was going on with Starr's family.

Speaking of Starr, the gorgeous spitfire came charging down the restaurant back steps now. He'd planned to have a "discussion" with her parents before she saw them, but apparently he hadn't dressed fast enough. Now things would be more complicated. Par for the course around Starr since the first day he'd done a double take, realizing his impish neighbor had grown into a bombshell.

He should have had the conversation with her earlier, but the risk had seemed too high given they were both half-dressed. He'd been too aware of her in that whispery thin T-shirt while he'd stood there only halfway finished dressing himself. Too easily memories from a year ago slid through his mind, how she'd sat on the edge of the tub and watched him shave. Not long after, he'd lifted her onto the sink and plunged himself deep inside her, her body already damp and ready for him.

Hell.

Clothes didn't seem to help much now since the wind played havoc with her gauzy sundress, plastering it to her body as she made her way across the lawn, sandals slapping her determination. He'd always enjoyed all that spunk and fire poured into the way they came together in bed.

They'd never had much luck resisting each other, another reason it was damn wise to meet out here on the lawn in open daylight rather than risk stepping into her carriage house. His leaving had hurt her last year. But *she* was the one who'd turned down his offer to try again. She could have come with him and he would have given her the world—shown her the world. Made love around the world.

But he had more pressing concerns than sex right now. Evicting Starr's family topped his list. "Good morning, babe."

She stopped dead in her tracks, her dress rustling around her legs, her mass of curls a swirl of motion, but then nothing about Starr ever stayed still. Well, except for the stubborn part of her that refused to leave this place.

Her toes curled in her shoes. Just that small motion stirred him because he knew. He affected her.

Then she turned, her eyes a sultry, dusky view that always sucker punched him. "Good morning to you, too. I see you're ready for work now."

Starr's voice washed over him like a surprise wave from the shore. She'd always had that effect on him— the only woman who'd ever had the power to linger in his thoughts.

Except he couldn't let her derail him now. "Actually, I'm heading over to give your family a wake-up call."

"That's where I'm going. They seem to be already moving about."

"I didn't mean that kind of wake-up." He stepped between her and the RVs, determined those people wouldn't hurt her any further.

"David, you don't need to worry." A sad smile strained her face as she swiped her windswept hair from her face. "Your mother and I have already spoken. I'm going to ask them to move off the grass and over to the beach."

A beach three states over wouldn't be enough to satisfy him. "That isn't what I meant. They need to leave."

"It isn't your place to make that call."

"You can't actually *want* them to stay."

"I'll handle them." Her chin tipped with a bravado he recognized from the day she'd arrived in the neighborhood, a grubby scrap of a kid with a mop of hair that likely hadn't seen a brush in a week. "I always do."

He resisted the urge to gather her in his arms,

knowing full well she wouldn't welcome the gesture. But he wasn't backing down. "You don't have to. I'll take care of this today. Now."

Her pretty lips went tight. "You don't have to and in case you missed out on noticing, I didn't ask for your help."

She may have been standing there steely strong, but he remembered well the teen who'd cried all over his chest because of how much damage these people could do with even a token visit when they attempted to lure her into their world again.

"David?"

He snapped back to the present. "Yes?"

"Step aside, please."

"No." Not a damn chance.

"No? Who the hell do you think you are to tell me no?" Her amazing hair seemed to crackle and lift with the energy overflow, as if her short and willowy body couldn't contain it all. "I realize you're embarrassed to have them in your precious prestigious neighborhood, but this is my property and I will take care of the issue."

He started to explain to her…then stopped. He didn't want her softening because then he'd do something risky…like touch her.

"We can stand here and debate this all day, but you know me well and once I've made up my mind…" David began to say.

"You don't budge." She fondled a glue gun tucked

halfway in her pocket. "It's not an endearing quality, you know."

Perhaps not, but it was one that would keep her safe.

Problem was, this woman was almost as stubborn as him. Almost.

So where did that leave him? Much more of this and he would have to do something like toss her over his shoulder and pass her off to her sister. Claire was the most logical woman he'd ever met. Surely he could garner an ally in her.

Starr stepped closer as if to brush past. His hands itched to touch her, even if only for a fireman's hold that would no doubt inflame her. God, she was hot when her temper flared.

Her pupils dilated with an awareness that could well send them both dashing back to her place. They wouldn't even have to get naked. They'd done it half-clothed often enough, coming together in a frenzy, too impatient to wait.

Then had come the slow, leisurely sex…

His breathing went ragged. His whole body tensed, muscles straining to be set loose and take this woman.

His cell phone buzzed in his jacket pocket. Damn.

It could only be work. He didn't have anything else in his life. He usually lived for the thrill of his job, but right now the thrill of this woman…

Just damn.

Stepping back, he reached into his coat and pulled out his phone to check the number. It could wait until he got into his car.

He shoved his cell back into his coat. "Starr, none of this changes what needs to happen with your family."

"And none of this changes the fact that my business, my life is not your problem." Her stubborn jaw jutted.

Without question, he would have to carry her off the lawn and lock her in her house, not exactly legal.

And then it hit him. He had a better way to circle around the situation after all. His connections at work. Find something on her family, because his radar, honed from assignments around the world, blared that they were always up to something, something that would spell bad news for Starr.

He nodded. "Believe whatever you want for why I want them gone, but I'm not done here. I'll be back to settle this later." He had to add, "Be careful."

David thumbed the remote control to his Lexus. The sooner he got to work, the sooner he could put out feelers about the Cimino family.

Just because Starr was hell-bent on her independence didn't mean he would stand back and let anyone take advantage of her.

Starr plunked her butt down on the back step of the Beachcombers Restaurant and stared at the Cimino family RVs from the quiet retreat of the deep porch. After her confrontation with David, she needed a moment to collect herself before she could handle another face-to-face with anyone—especially the residents of those three crumbling RVs.

The front of the restaurant hummed with activity from brunch traffic transitioning into lunch. Ashley worked the gift shop while studying for her CPA exam. The back section, which they used as a bar, wouldn't stir to life until suppertime and into the evening when the weekend's live band cranked to life, so she soaked up the second's silence to watch the shadows moving behind the gingham curtains covering the RV windows.

Her time to gather herself had come to an end.

The larger RV—the one towed behind a truck as opposed to the other two that were single units—rocked with walking bodies. Her stomach clenched. She'd seen her family only five times in the last seventeen years— this would make number six. And during each visit, they made their displeasure known when she hadn't fallen into line by returning to the "traveler clan" fold.

Aunt Libby's stolen silver flatware.

Mrs. Hamilton-Reis's Dutch tulips smashed by RV wheels.

David's keyed Mustang.

They knew how to hurt her most, through embarrassment. What would they do this time? Hard won control inched away.

A door swung wide. Ma filled the opening.

Gita had aged. The notion stabbed through Starr with a sympathy she didn't want and outright feared because it made her vulnerable, seeing those streaks of gray in her hair, the wrinkles lining her mother's face. Her ma still wore her hair long and curly like Starr, gathered in a ponytail, her jeans and shirt with fringe in constant motion, giving her a hummingbird air as she raced down the steps. "Good morning, sunshine."

More like *good afternoon,* but Starr wasn't going to start off the conversation by being contrary. "What brings all of you to the area?"

"Our baby girl of course," her father answered, standing on the top step, stretching his arms over his head.

No denying her parentage. She'd inherited her mother's hair, and her da's face and slight stature, which gave her a clear view into their home on wheels. Over his shoulders she could see the standard assortment of purses. Not that her ma collected purses in the manner of most fashion-conscious PTA moms. Nah. Gita Cimino collected purses *from* PTA moms.

Currently visible—a black sequined bag with a cell-phone caddy dangling and an oversize brown leather bag with diapers sticking out and a couple of bottles tucked into pouches along the side. Starr's heart squeezed as she thought about the poor young mother reporting her bag stolen while she jostled a hungry baby on her hip.

Gita and Frederick Cimino were a match made in hell.

The other two Cimino brothers and their wives had their own scams of choice. The older brother special-ized in items bought in bulk on the Internet and sold door to door—magic sweepers, garbage disposals, dishes, vitamins, herbal remedies. You name it, Starr figured he'd scammed it.

The youngest brother specialized in out-of-court set-tlements—slipping on a sidewalk, breaking a tooth in a restaurant, the list went on. She'd been roped into those many a time as a child because an injured kid evoked major sympathy.

Was it any wonder she'd been so jaded when at ten years old she'd clutched the social worker's hand and stood in front of Aunt Libby's looming double doors?

"So hey there, Starr," her mother called, making her way across the lawn. "No hug for your ma?"

"If you need one, then I'm over here."

Her mother hesitated mid hummingbird buzz across the lawn and perched her hands on her hips. "Still carrying a grudge, I see."

Starr stayed silent even though she wanted to speak. Nearly being killed by the woman after being stuck in the camper all day in the heat? Reasonable grudge material so far as she could tell.

While a very, very wise Frederick headed for a walk along the beach, Gita skimmed her way across the sandy lawn and took the Beachcomber steps more slowly. Starr could feel her skin tightening in fear of the hug…. Then Gita dropped to sit beside her, no fake semblance of familial affection, thank goodness, which showed an understanding of Starr's position. In that moment, Starr forgave her a little—or at least eased up on some of the anger.

She hadn't even known how much rage roiled inside her until she opened the tap to ease a cup free, almost like working an overfull keg at the bar. Could the rawness of her emotions be blamed on David's return?

Might as well make conversation, and the obvious questions needed asking after all. Heaven knew she needed to deal with them before David came charging over like a bull on a rampage. "What time did y'all pull in last night?"

"Around 3:00 a.m."

So she'd been deeply asleep by then, dead tired after closing up the restaurant. Still, she wondered how she'd missed the arrival of the caravan. It was ghostly spooky how they'd sneaked up on her. And David's return, too. The cosmos was ganging up on her today. "You must have better mufflers these days. I didn't even hear you."

"Your uncle Benny picked up a few extra, dirt cheap off the Internet." She stroked a seashell-encrusted stepping stone at the base of the stairs and by the covetous gleam in Gita's eyes, Starr knew where to look if it turned up missing tomorrow.

"I should have guessed. He's always got his eye out for those bulk bargains." When she'd been around nine, she'd helped him hawk encyclopedias. No matter to Benny that they were a decade out of date.

"Of course you didn't guess. You're getting rusty since you've been away from the family for so long." Gita shook her head and tutted, loosening a gray curl from the band. "It's to be expected since you're not with the family anymore."

Implied guilt? She refused to accept it.

So why couldn't she find her backbone? Time to rectify that now, as she'd told David she would. Not because she saw David's mother peering around her heavy brocade curtains, but because Starr wanted to regain control of her business, of her life before she weakened and leaned on David again.

"Ma, you'll need to tell the family to move the caravan over to the beach, so it's not visible from the road."

"Ah, we're bad for business parking in the lot like that." She nodded with surprising understanding and not a sign of censure. "Gives off the air of vagrants."

She hadn't expected it to be this easy or for her mother to be this blunt—or honest. "I don't mean to be insulting." She fished in her pocket and pulled out a folded piece of paper. "I've typed up a list of some beautiful waterside RV parks in the area that will accommodate your needs perfectly."

Her fist clenched around the paper while she waited—prayed—that her mother would take the list and hit the road.

"Baby, I'm not insulted. I understand about doing whatever it takes to bring in the buck. We'll get off your lawn and onto the beach over there. No worries or need to waste money on one of those parks. You've got a great view there and we'll situate ourselves just right, now that we know the angle you want us to work. We'll have vacationers stamped all over us by sundown."

"Hey, Ma, wait—"

"Shhh. Just listen." Gita slung her arm around Starr's

shoulders and pulled her in for that unwanted hug. "We can play roles well. We'll even beef up business for your little artsy gift shop as a personal favor. You'll see."

Starr stiffened even as her arm automatically slid around Ma's waist out of habit. Already she was falling back into old habits even though she'd told David not a half hour ago that she had a spine of steel. David. Why did all of her thoughts have to cycle back around to him?

This wasn't what she wanted at all. She wanted them out of sight. Actually, she wanted them gone before their con games and get-rich schemes caused trouble in town. Aside from the fact that she couldn't condone their crimes, she also couldn't bear these reminders of the gypsy child she'd been. A member of a traveler clan not worthy of David. How had the conversation shifted from having them out of sight to them poking their sticky fingers into her business?

The metaphorical beer keg exploded and she didn't have a clue how to stop the spewing mess of her emotions.

Three

Standing in her parents' RV doorway with stars glinting overhead at the end of one of those endless days, Starr passed the bags full of chicken wings and everything else she could think of to feed the gang supper. Hopefully this would keep them happily settled inside for the night.

Her aunt Essie—Uncle Benny's wife—shuffled off the Styrofoam boxes of food to the mini counter by the sink, pushing aside a Crock-Pot.

"Come on in and join us," Aunt Essie offered in that fake Bostonian accent she affected in an effort to claim she was a down-on-her-luck member of *the* Kennedy clan. She actually thought a few touch-football games on the lawn would convince people. "We would love the chance to hear all about your fancy new business."

"Thanks, really, but I've already eaten…." Starr backed off the last step—into air. She'd been swooped off her feet by someone.

A man.

Her stomach lurched as her brain caught up to the fact that a muscular arm banded around her waist. The scent of salty ocean breeze, expensive soap and…exotic *man* wafted up to her nose.

One man in particular.

David hefted her closer against his chest, his breath hot and bearing a hint of toothpaste against her ear. "Good night, ma'am," he said nodding to the crowd snatching containers of food. "Starr has other plans for supper this evening."

Pivoting without waiting for a response, he charged toward the beach with long strides. Away from his house. From her house. Away from the people scattered along the dock pitching shells into the ocean or making out under the moonbeams.

"Care to clue me in on the other plans?" Starr wriggled in his grasp. He hitched her higher, up over his shoulder in a fireman's hold. "I'm not enjoying these plans."

Well, perhaps she was a little interested and fired up as she grabbed hold of his waist to steady herself. Then she figured she shouldn't let him know she'd given up quite so easily. She kicked her feet in midair and managed to land two good thunks that elicited a grunt if not a more satisfactory outright ouch. "David, put me down."

"No." He kept right on walking, hitching her higher.

She gritted her teeth against the image of her family crowding the door of the RV, Aunt Essie and Uncle Benny side by side, watching while others peered through the windows. Jeez. Couldn't they just eat their supper, for heaven's sake?

"This is not the way to win me over." The macho show of force should have torqued her off, and it would have if she could think through the haze of shimmering hormones. The fine weave of his cotton button-down rubbed against her bargain-bin buy. She'd never been a clothes horse—more of a sales-rack and Goodwill-find shopper—but her tactile artist's senses appreciated the decadent fabrics a man like David wore.

"Who said I wanted to win you over?" he asked without missing a step.

Now that landed an ouch to *her* ego—and momentarily stalled her kicking. "Will you please tell me where we're going and why you're doing this?"

"Soon."

His timing. Always on his timetable, all or nothing.

At least she would get to know where he was taking her. And if she was lucky, she would get to push him into the ocean right afterward as payback for these he-man tactics that—damn him—really were kind of turning her on as she thought of other times he'd carried her over his shoulder only to toss her on a bed, or down onto the sand. Then he would make his way from the foot of the bed paying passionate attention to every inch of her body.

His feet thudded along the pier outside his house, abandoned. Apparently he planned to have their late night conversation out here.

Alone.

She was in trouble. Maybe she could jump in the ocean if she didn't like the path of their chat.

David set her down slowly, sensually easing her body along his until he leaned her against the dock's railing, the bulk of his height blocking out everything but him as he stood in front of her. His pants had stayed perfectly pressed even after a full day of work. His cotton shirt she'd so enjoyed rubbing against bore the slightest wrinkle from the press of her body against him when he'd carried her. Something about the faint wrinkle hinted at an intimacy that tingled through her. Her gaze fell to his arms, his sleeves rolled up, dark hair along his forearms. Strong arms.

Ohhh-kay. Time to shift her attention elsewhere. She looked up to his face. The moonlight cast shadows over his scowl.

She wanted to kiss that grumpy expression right off his face…except…oh, yeah…she was mad at him. God, she forgot that so easily when the sparks started snapping between them.

Starr bit her bottom lip to keep her words and kisses locked up tight. He'd started this. She wouldn't give him the satisfaction of begging for an answer. She'd begged often enough around this man—in bed.

The pupils of his eyes widened. Could he read her thoughts now, too? Was he that good of an interrogator at work? Would she be allowed no secrets from him?

Finally, he blinked. She exhaled.

He tunneled his hand through her curls and cupped the back of her head. "Starr, babe, I thought we went over this earlier today. You've got to stay away from them."

His touch muddled her thoughts when doggone it, she had a list of things, logical things, she wanted to say, such as this wasn't his problem or any of his business, and instead she found herself babbling, "I've asked them to leave and go to an RV park. They refused. Short of siccing the cops on them, I don't know what more I can do to move them."

"Then call the police." His fingers massaged hypnotic circles beyond anything her ma could have set up in one of her psychic scams. "Or evict them. They have no legal right to be here if you don't want them around."

Starr chewed on her lip again. She really should tell him to get his hand off her, but it felt so amazingly good and she'd never been particularly strong when it came to resisting his touch….

The very reason she had to stop this. Now. She gripped his wrist. "David. Stop."

She held his gaze in a battle of wills, the heat of his skin radiating through even his rolled-up shirt cuff.

Finally, his fingers slowed against her scalp and he swung his arm away, to his side. She released his wrist—and the gulp of air in her lungs.

He tugged at his tie as if in need of air, too. "Damn it, Starr, they steal from people, they prey on the weak and they're undoubtedly trying to prey on you."

"I'm too strong to let anything happen." And she was stronger now, thanks to the self-confidence Aunt Libby had given her. "They'll hang out for a few days, realize I don't have any money to give them and then they'll leave. Just like always."

His eyes narrowed. "I can make it happen faster than that."

Too easily she could let him deal with her problems, but she couldn't tangle her life with his again. "No offense to your professional buddies, but don't you think that has been tried again and again? It never works. They always get away with whatever illegal or squirrelly scam they're running."

Technically not true, she had to confess, at least to herself.

The police had caught up with them one time. The summer they had found ten-year-old Starr locked alone in a boiling hot RV for eight hours while her parents had gone door to door collecting money for yet another bogus charity. She'd nearly died of heatstroke. Five days in the hospital later, the child protective services in Charleston, South Carolina, had placed her with Aunt Libby as a foster child.

At first she'd been wary of Aunt Libby. Nobody could be that nice. Slowly, Aunt Libby's maternal magic had worn through the years of neglect and abuse and Starr had begun to heal.

Then had come a new fear—that her family would try to take her back.

Thank God, Aunt Libby had always known just how to handle them on their rare visits to the seaside mansion, always with their hands out. And today, Starr followed Aunt Libby's model of brushing them off.

"Starr?" David snapped his fingers in front of her face, his voice urgent, a hint impatient.

"What, David? Can we make this quick? I need to get back to work." Actually back to Ashley's party, due to start up in an hour.

"Has your family ever been reported to *me?*"

"What do you mean?"

"Has anyone ever told *me* the specifics of their recent scams?" He thumped his chest.

"Well, uh, I guess technically not." She knew he was darned amazing at his job. Heaven knew his mother bragged about his feats often enough. The woman hadn't wanted the two of them together, yet she also hadn't been able to resist rubbing Starr's nose in what a "catch" she'd missed out on as he sent postcards from this country or that.

Little did his proud mama know those far flung travels only cemented Starr's resolution she'd made the right choice. Her connection to Aunt Libby's crumbling old antebellum home, this city, the sisters of her heart went deeper than David could understand.

"David, honestly, I'm not in their inner circle these days since they know I'm not into that kind of life. Even if I were in the know on their plans, they're so darn slippery in the execution."

"No one gets past me."

His confidence was unmistakable.

She couldn't resist jabbing. "Could that be because your enormous ego blocks the doorway?"

His mouth twitched. God, she loved his mouth, those perfectly full lips that brought such pleasure. His ability to laugh at himself made him all the more attractive.

"You always have been the only woman who wouldn't put up with my crap."

David smoothed his hand over her head again, his fingers tangling in her curls as he slid farther this time, down her neck, her back, free of her hair to palm her waist. He flattened her body to his in one of those masterful shows of gentle force that sent her senses tingling even as she longed to stomp on his foot.

He tucked his size-fourteen wingtip shoes gently over the toes of her feet in a preemptive move as if reading her thoughts. "You may be the only woman who doesn't put up with my crap, but you're also the only woman I can't seem to forget."

Darn him. He always did know what to say to melt her like the glue sticks in her arts-and-crafts gun. His foot slipped off her feet so she could arch on her toes to receive the kiss she could already sense coming.

No. She would hold strong against temptation.

She flattened her hands to his shoulders to stop his kiss, if not the embrace. Their chests pumped for air against each other in time with the gushing waves below the dock.

"I have to go," Starr gasped. "We're having a surprise graduation party for Ashley."

His arms stayed banded around her, his chin resting on top of her head. He stood a full foot taller than her, yet their bodies always seemed to fit. "No way can she be that old already."

"A lot of time has passed since you and I were together." Years that had filled his body with muscles and her heart with resolve of what she needed from life.

But oh, how she couldn't push away from this man just yet. She'd resisted the kiss. She could indulge in at least this much.

"A year."

She'd meant since their teenage time together, since they'd had a relationship. "Does that really count? That was just—" incredible, heart-searing "—sex."

That she could narrow down the experience to one word was truly an injustice to a weekend that had left her seeing stars for days.

"And your point is?"

"We don't have anything else in common." Her heart pinched tight at the minor lie. They'd had plans in common, once upon a dream ago. Of course, now they'd plotted their lives and their paths diverged. Still, pushing him away again was tougher than she'd expected. Damn it, why did this have to ache all over again? "I can't see past your eyes anymore but I'll be honest and lay it all out there and say you hurt me. And quite frankly, between you and the gypsy circus act parked on my lawn, I've reached my hurt quota for one lifetime."

If only he would step back and give her space, she could breathe. And yet that traitorous part of her craved his touch. All the more reason she needed to make this break fast.

"Well, babe, while I'm not sure I like being lumped in with a bunch of crooks, I get your point." His hands fell to rest on her shoulders, a warm and too-tempting weight that spurred her to press harder.

She inhaled a bracing breath full of his tantalizing scent. "So while I understand that you have to settle your mother's health issues, you will stay clear of me while you're here." She tipped her chin toward each of his hands still cupping her shoulders. "I don't want us to repeat past mistakes."

This was tough enough—having him touch her, here where they'd once made love under an eiderdown comforter he'd dragged down to the beach behind a dune, back when the place had been less populated.

He raised his hands and backed away. "No past mistakes."

Starr wrapped her arms around her waist to ward off a chill that shouldn't have stood a chance on such a warm spring night. As she watched him lumber away, she let herself take one final moment to enjoy the view before she shook herself back into reality, a reality that would not include him.

Except wait. A dangerous realization tickled up her spine.

He may have said no past mistakes, but Special Agent Word Craftsman had never once agreed to stay away from her.

He was ticked off.

David stood on the outer edge of Ashley's farewell party held in the Beachcombers Bar and watched as everyone celebrated the youngest sister's summa cum laude success. His hand clutched around the gift he'd bought, his mind locked on his earlier conversation with Starr. He'd been pushed for time to find Ashley a gift but being here was important for more than one reason.

How could Starr just call it sex? He might be arrogant…

Might be? He could almost hear Starr's throaty laughter in his ear.

Fine. He had his fair share of ego. He had to be confident in his job, believe in his decisions and forge ahead without hesitation because a moment's flinch could get him killed. Or worse yet, cost someone else's life.

But back to the original source of his frustration. It had never been "just sex" with him and Starr, otherwise they could have figured out how to be "just friends" a long time ago. Otherwise, he wouldn't make a point of avoiding her during times he spent at his condo in downtown Charleston.

Sure, he was gone on assignment often, around the U.S. and overseas, but he spent more time in the city than she knew. Because *he* knew the more they saw each other, the more he risked hurting her again.

Why hadn't some smart guy snapped her up yet?

Some smart guy David already hated with every ridiculous dog-in-the-manger fiber of his being. Hell. David planted his feet in the sawdust-covered floor to keep from barging ahead and claiming her now. He knew he wasn't right for her. She'd made that clear enough. That didn't mean he could stand the thought of her with someone else.

So if he was avoiding her, what was he doing standing on the outskirts of Ashley's graduation party with a present in hand?

Because he wanted to keep himself between her and her scam-artist family. A quick glance showed him that lights blazed inside all three of the RVs. He shifted his attention back to the party and saw only a cluster of around fifty people. The bar floor sported a mix of college students, Citadel cadets and some friends of Claire and Starr's from their clientele, most of whom came from the local Charleston Air Force Base.

David scanned the room and finally found Ashley parked over by the leaning remains of a hacked-up tiered strawberry cake. Starr must have made it specially for her little sister because Starr preferred mint chocolate. A part of him resented that he knew that and a thousand more details about Starr, minute facts that packed his brain and refused to fade.

He inched into the room, flattening his way along the wall until he made it over to the guest of honor, who seemed to prefer to take her congratulations one at a time rather than en masse.

Tall and willowy, Ashley leaned against a support pole, her ever-present long ponytail draped over one shoulder as if to hide the slight remains of her scoliosis.

"Hey there, little sister." He tugged the tail of her auburn hair, kid-sis style. "You're quite the queen of the ball, tonight."

"I would have just as soon gone out to dinner, the three of us girls, but you know my sisters."

"A bit pushy and a lot proud." He let go of her hair. "You're thoughtful to go along with their plan."

"I love them."

His mother would have been shocked to know he envied the camaraderie shared by a houseful of dirt-poor foster girls without a lineage paper worth speaking of between them. Granted, the loner quality had honed him into a stronger agent, but as a kid, he'd watched through his window for years.

Only one female had dared defy his mother and cross the boundary line between the houses to say hello to the boy next door. Starr feared nothing.

So why did she balk at sending away the people from her past parked outside? What hold did they have over her?

All of which he needed to stop thinking about for now. This was Ashley's night.

He started to congratulate the graduate on her summa cum laude grades, but she'd been lured away by someone else wanting to pass along good wishes. He simply set his gift beside the cake and headed back to his perch by the door—

And bumped into a burly blond wall of two men. He recognized Vic Jansen, a lumberjack-looking fellow in flannel and jeans, a veterinarian who'd married Claire last year. Having that big lug around provided an extra level of protection. David would do well to cultivate a friendship with the man.

Time to quit thinking like a lone wolf, a habit ingrained in him growing up as an only child. "Good evening. Sorry I haven't had a chance to come over and say hello since I got back in town."

"No problem. Between work and the baby, I don't see daylight in the yard all that much myself." Vic gestured to the blond giant next to him. "Meet my cousin, Seth Jansen. We finally lured him from out west to join the family here. He bought that small airport ten miles down the road."

"Really?" His curiosity upped a notch. "I hadn't heard it was up for sale."

"It wasn't. I closed on the deal a month ago." Seth Jansen had obviously come straight from work, still in his suit pants and white button-down shirt, sleeves rolled up his only concession for the casual party atmosphere.

"Welcome to town. So you'll be living here in one of Beachombers' B-and-B rooms?"

Damn, but jealousy chomped hard on a man's hide. David waited for the answer.

"Yes, while I finish building a place of my own out by the airport."

Vic hooked his thumbs in the back pockets of his jeans. "I gotta admit, I appreciate the extra set of eyes around here with our new residents parked out back. Seth and I are working swing shifts so one of us is always around to keep an eye on the women."

Of course. David resolved to put his libido on hold. He'd been glad to have Vic around, but then of course Vic would always have the safety of his wife and child first and foremost in his mind—as it should be. Adding Seth to the protective detail significantly increased their odds of keeping Starr safe. And now that Ashley had finished college, they had another female to worry about.

Hell, he needed to get rid of the Cimino squatters ASAP. He'd done all he could at work to set the investigative wheels in motion. Now he needed to create a protective detail on site. And these men were valuable assets.

Four

Starr wiped down the bar for the thirty-first time. The darn thing was clean and she knew it. The whole place was spotless and empty of guests, Ashley's celebration complete.

Vic and Claire were upstairs in their second-floor living quarters with baby Libby. Starr couldn't find it in her to begrudge them their happiness. Claire had struggled hard to learn to let down her barriers and embrace love. And poor Vic had lost a daughter in a drowning accident before he'd moved here. His first wife had blamed him for no good reason and divorced him shortly thereafter. But Vic was a great guy who deserved the happiness he'd found.

And Seth? The big lug was a hunk, no question. She would have to be comatose not to notice. However, even having him reside in one of the third-floor quarters didn't offer the least temptation. She simply wasn't attracted to lumbering blond guys. Or red-haired men.

Or even *most* dark-haired guys, for that matter.

Her attention seemed stuck on *one* particular man with jet-black hair and a mansion-sized ego. Starr hitched a hip against the bar and stared out past the porch to the dock where David stood silhouetted at the end of the pier, staring outward pensively.

She recalled from past conversations that he said the water offered him the perfect place for concentrating, sorting through problems. The water drew him. He'd sailed competitively throughout the U.S. and even in Europe—as long as it hadn't interfered with his soccer playing. He'd wanted to compete professionally but his mother had found that too plebian.

Off he'd gone to college on a joint soccer and academic scholarship to circumvent his mother's power and money altogether—and taken a public service job, his dream, not his family's. The house and half the money, however, had become his at twenty-one because of his father's will, regardless of his horrified mother's wishes.

Now David answered to no one.

Starr wadded the rag in her fist, clutching it to her aching stomach. No doubt, the complexity of this man called to her.

Her gaze drifted to wicker baskets filled with gifts for

Ashley. David's rested right on top. A satiny backpack in the bright pinks Ashley loved, but ergonomic to accommodate her spinal problems. Big purses and briefcases left her already-out-of-whack vertebrae aching. It took a man completely comfortable in his masculinity to pick out magenta anything.

And his present for Ashley meant more to Starr than if he'd bought her a hothouse full of roses or some hefty gift certificate.

He deserved a decent thank you.

Starr pitched the soggy rag into the sink behind the bar and made her way down the steps, across the lawn and along the planked dock. She couldn't help herself. She reached to pull free the hair band restraining her curls and tried, tried, tried to tell herself she shook her hair loose because her head ached from the tight restraint. But she knew deep inside, a part of her enjoyed the fact that David liked her hair down. And darn it, even if her clothes—shirt and a shirt made of many scarves— might be rumpled from the long party, she would indulge in this small vanity to look that bit better in front of an old boyfriend.

Each step closer to David pulled the tension tighter in her stomach, too much like the days when she'd watched from her room for him to step from his house and gesture for her to join him. An instant later she would slip free for a 2:00 a.m. walk along the shoreline while they shared dreams and kisses. She shouldn't still want a simple conversation with him so much.

But she did.

Starr slowed to a stop beside him, careful not to let so much as her flowing scarf top brush against his suit that cost more than she made in a month. "You're still here."

He shifted to face her, leaning back on his elbows. "I could have been anyone lurking around." His white shirt shone like a beacon in the dark, his suit jacket draped over the dock rail, his tie tucked in the coat pocket, his top two buttons open to reveal a patch of throat she longed to kiss—holy cow he was that much closer to out of his clothes.

David blinked, slowly, sensually. "You should be more careful. I don't like your being alone at closing."

"I'm not alone." She forced words past her lips only half-aware of what she said, her body more in tune with the angle of his legs, his arms, the rise and fall of his chest, the widening of his pupils darkening his eyes. "Vic's upstairs. Seth, too. They're a simple shout away if I need them."

"And does Vic walk you over to the carriage house after closing?" He paused for a slow blink, then angled closer, possessively. "Does this new guy—Seth?"

David couldn't be jealous, could he? "First off, I don't need a man to be my keeper. Second of all, I'm only walking across my own lawn. And third of all—"

"You run a bar and you're hot. What if some drunk—"

"I carry a can of Mace and I have taken a self-defense class—" Hey, had he just paid her a compliment in there? Something about being hot. She indulged in a quick shiver of pleasure before she continued, "You'll have to accept it when I say that I'm a careful adult. Thank you for being concerned."

"And butt out." His mouth tipped in a one-sided smile made all the more devilish by the stars glinting off his dark hair.

"I didn't say it." She shook her head, her curls teasing her shoulders.

"You didn't have to. I hear you loud enough." His smile faded "Where's your Mace?"

"Fine. I forgot my purse with my Mace tonight because you've shot my concentration to hell. There. Are you satisfied?" She hated the bobble in her voice. "David, I don't want to argue with you anymore. We're going to bump into each other for years to come—or until you sell your mother's big old house. Can't we find a way to be polite to each other without ending up in bed?"

That silenced him for seven sloshes of the waves against the dock. He reached, looped an arm around her waist and pulled her against his chest, holding her loosely, his chin resting on her head. "I'm not sure."

There was such a familiarity in the way he touched her. Could it simply be because they'd known each other such a long time? Each time she saw him, she resolved she would handle things differently, establish distance, and yet they fell right back into their old patterns of physical ease around each other. Time after time, she tortured herself by allowing touches that couldn't lead anywhere.

Except last year…

Starr stood still, their only contact his hands on her back, his chin on her hair, but ah, she could feel him catching her scent in a primal way. "It was considerate of you to bring Ashley a gift, and such a thoughtful one, too." Sure it was just a backpack, something that likely didn't put a dent in his abundant portfolio, but the time and thought expended were far more valuable.

"You taught me how to pick a gift that fits the person rather than something generic." A wicked smile of reminiscence creased his tanned features. "I never expected to have roses pitched back in my face."

Well, whoa. That tossed cold water on her kissing memories. She tipped back to smile up in his face and let her arms slide to loop around his back in return. "I did *not* throw them back in your face."

"No. Worse yet," he continued, oddly enough not seeming in the least angry. Rather amused. "You sent them to my mother with a card labeling them From a Secret Admirer. My poor mother freaked out thinking she had a stalker."

She settled into the memory with him. "At least you finally got that German shepherd you always wanted."

"Günter was a damn good dog." He paused for the first time with a sentimentality that caught her unaware. However, before she could reach out to offer any sense of comfort, he continued, "Then I tried again with those chocolates that cost my whole allowance because, contrary to popular belief, my mother didn't let me spend whatever I wanted."

What? She hadn't known that. She felt pretty bad now as she remembered passing out the Godivas like lemon drops at lunch at school. Except afterward he'd watched her more closely and *that* was cool. Then he'd figured out how much she'd enjoyed her art class. The tubes of paint made into a bouquet of flowers had totally won her over.

She'd pulled him behind the lockers and plastered a kiss on him that even the memory could have melted those paints had she been holding them today.

How could he be so Cro-Magnon and thoughtful all at once? That dichotomy had kept her in his bed far longer than had been wise for her heart. All the more reason to leave now because, heaven help her, her heart pounded in her chest so hard surely he could hear. Her quick breaths matched his and knowing he wanted her every bit as much as she wanted him upped the ante to sheer torture.

"Enough, David, that's all I wanted to say. Thank you, I mean. It's late and I should turn in. Morning comes too fast. I hope everything is okay with your mother."

"Fine. Good night." He slid one hand free to click off the dock light.

She should pull away before she did something silly like arch up to press a thank-you kiss on one side of his mouth and a goodbye kiss on the other side. And hey, that felt so good open-mouthed kiss smack dab…

His arms were tightening around her and dreams had

somehow become a reality with his tongue sweeping a deep and strong possession, his hands palming her back to press her breasts against his solid chest. Always, always his touch worked a perfect blend of yes, just like that and please, please more...

Her hands crawled up his back, the thin cotton of his shirt offering too little barrier to keep out the heat of him. Too much barrier when she wanted to touch skin.

Bad idea. Bad idea. *Bad* idea.

But sweet mercy, she was going to do it anyway. Just a sweep of hard, muscular pecs to give her something to dream about. She skimmed her hands around front to find buttons and made fast work down them until she could touch his chest, feel the gentle abrasion of hair and skin. Muscles pulled tight under her exploration, answering her with an affirmation of want.

She'd been so busy indulging herself that she'd almost forgotten about David's hand. An oversight he fixed for her in a hurry as his fingers wandered down her leg with deceptive slowness. Long, lazy fingers. Her heartbeat quickened.

He slipped his hands under her skirt, up to cup her buttocks and lift her so she meshed torso to torso against him, her feet dangling in midair. He left her with no choice but to trust him, trust his strength to keep her safely in place while they kissed and writhed against each other. Her flesh heated unbearably, her whole body sensitized until she could even feel the kiss of saltwater on the breeze.

Heaven help her, it would be so easy to raise her legs and wrap them around his waist as she'd done often enough. And before she knew it, her legs locked around him with a sweet familiarity.

A simple flick of her hand would open his fly and release the steely length of heat she felt against her belly. She wore a thong, so it wouldn't take much for him to slide aside her panties and plunge inside. But she couldn't bring herself to take that step.

Even thinking of it though, her body throbbed—begged—for the release he could bring her. It had been so long. She needed this. Needed him. A whimper escaped her. A whimper that sounded remarkably like a whispered *please*.

Please?

That lone word brought her back to the present. She would never let herself be so swayed by this man or any man again. She'd grown up at the mercy of her parents. Control over her own life meant everything to her.

With more than a little regret and an ache clear down to her toes, Starr slid her legs from around his waist and down to the dock. Given their height difference, gravity took care of the rest, pulling her lips free from his. Too bad she could still feel the heat of him on her mouth, the taste of him swirling through her.

With shaking hands she straightened her skirt, fingers plucking at the fabric. Why did something so wonderful have to be so wrong for her? She *knew* that being with David inevitably led to hurt. What would make her think now could be any different?

Nothing. She had nothing to go on. And damn, but that made her want to cry, which was dangerous because she just kept picturing that thoughtful pink backpack present for Ashley.

Starr backed away. "Thank you for coming by the party and thank you for worrying about my parents. You're good at taking care of people. You're a good man. But really, we're okay. We three sisters have been looking out for ourselves for a long time. Granted, dealing with my parents can be tough, but I need to do this. You won't always be here. So where does that leave me if I only know how to lean on you?"

He stayed silent though she took some small comfort from the fact that he seemed to struggle for the next breath almost as hard as she did.

"Exactly," she said sadly, wondering why she'd almost hoped he would have a quick rebuttal. She backed another step on shaking legs and then another, none of them far enough to cool the heat still searing through her at just his simple eyes on her body. "Goodbye, David."

Starr's farewell still ringing in his ears two hours later, David dropped to lounge against the wooden rail of his veranda, a glass of Scotch in his hand—a poor substitute for what he really wanted to be holding right now.

The moon shot a road of light across the ocean, so straight and simple. He'd stared at that often as a teen, planning his escape from this place. But he hadn't bargained on leaving alone.

His gaze shifted over to Starr's carriage house, all lights off where she now no doubt slept.

Starr. In bed. Naked.

A recipe for his insanity if ever there'd been one. David scratched behind his ear as if to shake loose that thought enough so he could function better.

And all the things that came after.

Still, he had an obligation to see this through. Find out what had brought her parents here and see them on their way. Once he knew Starr was safe, he could return to his normal life. In fact, he had a kick-ass assignment in Turkey coming up within the next two weeks.

Too bad Starr was so damn resistant to travel after her childhood. The artist within her would really get off on the rainbow display of tapestries to be found even in a simple row of street vendors.

He even had the perfect means of transportation for private, personal use at his fingertips now.

Talking with the Jansen cousins at the party, he'd found out more about Vic's cousin Seth. Apparently the guy was a pilot, small craft sort, who'd invented a must-have security device for airports to help combat attacks on planes during take-off and landing. He's registered the patent and made a mint.

Gotta admire the entrepreneurial spirit combined with making a major difference for his country.

Now he'd bought a local airport to set up search and

rescue operation in conjunction with a retired Air Force Special Ops guy, Rick DeMassi.

An idea sparked in David's mind. Why wait? He'd been approaching this problem with keeping Starr safe all wrong. He eyed the RVs full of bloodsucking leeches planning God only knew what this go round. No question, he needed to put distance between her and her family. And if he couldn't uproot them in a timely fashion, why not move Starr?

What better way than to entice her to go away with him?

Already he could hear her shriek of outrage, but he could overcome that. He swayed the toughest of people for a living and, quite frankly, given Starr's response last night, she wouldn't take that much persuasion.

He couldn't keep his hands off her and the feeling appeared mutual. Maybe they needed to get this out of their systems once and for all. And if they managed that very far away from South Carolina while his people in the office did a little unofficial investigation of her parents, then all the better.

He had a line on a nurse to watch over his mother. Nothing held him here. Talking Claire into letting Starr take a couple of days off would be the easiest part of the plan. Mamma Bear Claire would want Starr away from the Cimino Caravan as much as he did.

So, now all he had left to do was figure out what place would best entice Starr to fly away from all her worries and persuade her to go for it. But surely someone with his skills wouldn't have a problem with one five-foot-tall artist.

A petite bombshell artist who'd evaded him for a decade.

Five

No worries, Starr reassured herself. It was a new day.

Kneeling behind the cash-register counter, she pulled out a stack of hand-painted T-shirts to restock the shelves and resolved to be more optimistic. She'd stood her ground with David. No more *falling* back into old habits of falling into bed. She would put him in the past once and for all so she could move forward.

Much like she needed to put the Ciminos in her past?

Starr thunked down on her butt with the stack of shirts in her lap, her hand sketching over the inventory for extra gift-shop goodies. She might appear busy to the casual observer, but man, she was way gone in daydream land.

She had to stop short at placing David in the same category as her unfeeling, thieving relatives because, truth be told, she shared good memories with David. Amazing memories.

He deserved a slot in the sentimental file, even if placing him there gave him sway over her emotions now. She refused to deny the happiness they'd shared. To do so would be unfair, especially after he'd made her feel special when she'd spent so much of her life feeling like not just a second-class citizen, but somewhere around seventy-second class.

She also had to give him credit for helping her possess the confidence to pull off this business venture when she'd first had the inkling to present the notion to her sisters after Aunt Libby's will had been read and they'd realized the old house was theirs. And wow, who would have thought three girls with barely a penny between them could have turned a crumbling old Southern beachside mansion into a booming restaurant?

Business grew stronger by the day. The traffic now buzzed past, shepherded in for brunch by the extra help she and her sisters had been able to hire in the past months. Their success had been a real coup for a restaurant and bar that had only been in business for a couple of years. They'd even had enough cashflow this year to renovate the third floor for boarders or vacationing guests.

Their lunch and bar crowd came mostly from the military base and college community. Their supper clientele and parties catered to the wealthy interested in having their event in a historic Charleston beach home.

Having the large marina next door helped, as well, although there were some who wanted to turn that marina into a more sleek venture. Beachcombers had survived a number of buyout attempts from people who'd wanted to turn the stretch of land into condominiums. She and her sisters could have made a mint. But this business was about more than just staying together. It was about holding on to the only home, the only real sense of family the three of them had ever known.

Being a part of a growing legacy totally rocked and she never intended to take that for granted. No matter that David had tried to lure her into roaming the world with him during some of his less classified gigs as an OSI special agent. The enticing offer warred mightily with her desire for roots. Why couldn't he compromise?

Starr tossed a couple of the painted seashell ornaments on top of the shirt stack and rose.

And froze.

She sniffed once, twice. And yes. Her senses were right on. She would recognize her mother's over-applied cologne anywhere.

Starr peered around the side of the hostess station and sure enough Gita was checking things out with an attention to detail that went beyond curiosity. She wasn't stuffing her pockets, so Starr kept her peace and just watched rather than instigate a conversation. She would find out more this way anyhow.

Gita picked up the debit card machine, played around with the numbers for a moment, not that it would make a difference since she hadn't swiped a card, then shifted her attention to swishing her hand along a dangling line of necklaces as if playing an instrument.

Apparently bored, she made her way back to the door to—omigod—the rest of the family

So much for positive thinking. What were the odds that her family and David's mother would all decide they wanted brunch at the same time? And did they all have to wedge themselves through the double doors at once while the waitresses were occupied? The towering lobby seemed to shrink, oxygen definitely in short supply.

She'd never had a panic attack before, but she suspected her first might be well on its way.

Then it hit her. They had different dining rooms downstairs. She would simply place David's mother in her regular area—yes, for some bizarre reason the woman frequented Beachcombers for meals—and pray she didn't hit the buffet at the same time as Aunt Essie and company.

Of course that meant Starr would have to talk to David's cranky, judgmental mom, while keeping her eyes on the line to stage the right moments to set her free to fill her plate without running into the Ciminos. This would be pretty much like the mini-circus act her uncle Hugo had tried to offer schools. She'd broken her wrist trying to learn to ride a unicycle.

But she wasn't a defenseless child now.

Starr dumped the shirts and ornaments on a shelf and sprinted for Ashley over by the kitchen door. "Please, please, please take care of my relatives. Seat them at table thirteen. And tell them that's the number. They'll love it. They're into spurning superstitions." Starr monitored the incoming guests' progress. "I'll take care of Alice Hamilton-Reis."

The older woman had a way of leveling those censuring sniffs and glares at Ashley that made the younger girl draw into herself. But not on Starr's watch.

Ashley swept her long red hair back into a scrunchie as if preparing for a sweaty ordeal. "Are you sure you don't want to swap? I'll be glad to take on the old bat for you."

Starr's heart swelled at even the offer and what it no doubt cost shy Ashley to make. Sister love was a special thing.

"No, really. I'm going to manage her so she's out of the flow of traffic." She felt a pinch of scruples, too—which really bugged her. "Besides, David's worried about her health and the last thing I want on my conscience is to have her stroke out in the middle of her hash-brown casserole because the Ciminos tried to snitch her wallet."

"I really can handle her," Ashley insisted with a thread of steel in her voice Starr had never heard before. Maybe she needed to take a second glance at her baby sister who'd just graduated from college, not so much of a baby anymore.

Later though and she wouldn't make a test run on the theory with Mrs. Hamilton-Reis. Old Alice had more steamroller impact than all the Ciminos combined when she wanted, and Ashley…well…she'd been fragile for a long time. "I appreciate the gesture, but this is one ghost I'll take on by myself. Okay?"

Ashley reached to hug her sister in a fast embrace. "Good luck."

"Thanks, sweetie." Hey, it wasn't as if she were going to the gallows. Was she?

Starr glanced over her shoulder and saw Mrs. Hamilton-Reis making her way to the hostess station, her gaze cutting ever so slightly toward the Ciminos straggling behind her. Time to make an end run.

Starr patted Ashley on the back and they charged ahead. She listened to how her younger sister's quiet voice somehow cut through the babbling mayhem of the mass of chatter as she guided them to the left, leaving Starr alone with her charge.

"Good morning, Mrs. Hamilton-Reis. Would you like your regular seat by the window?"

She didn't understand why the woman came over so often when she obviously disapproved of the place and constantly complained about the food—after she ate. It was an odd dance they did, the aging lady griping, Starr always giving her a complimentary twenty percent off in recompense.

"Of course." She hitched her purse into the crook of her elbow, the same designer black leather bag Starr had seen the woman carry for as long as she could remember.

As Starr wove her way around tables of diners, she

CATHERINE MANN69

wondered what had happened to make the woman so sour. Surely something like that didn't happen in a vacuum. People had reasons for their attitudes.

And her parents? Aunts and uncles? That was a tougher nut to crack because of the way they skirted the law. At least Mrs. Hamilton-Reis wasn't a crook, and she had brought up a strong son.

"Here's your regular table. The flowers are fresh since the warm snap brought an early bloom to our azalea bushes," Starr offered up in an honest attempt to connect, since David's mother lived and breathed for her garden.

Now probably wasn't a good time to remember how she and Claire had sneaked out one night and trimmed—okay, mutilated—tea rosebushes into the shape of hooks and arrows because the woman had made little Ashley cry for snapping a bloom off her magnolia tree. The darn thing had been right on the property-line border after all.

"They're a lovely shade of pink," Mrs. Hamilton-Reis acceded, while straightening the silverware in subtle censorship, which totally negated the compliment. Not surprising. That was her way after all.

What had it been like for David to grow up in that kind of negative atmosphere? How odd she'd never considered that before, instead simply thinking of him as the pampered, beloved heir.

Mrs. Hamilton-Reis settled in her seat, arranged her napkin in her lap with exaggerated care, taking her time even to glance over the menu, though she always chose the buffet, and finally she set down the plastic-covered specials of the day. "So I see those people are still here in spite of my advice."

Reaching into the back pocket of her jeans, Starr gripped the tiny pad of paper and pencil for taking orders. Pencil poised, she tried not to snap it in two. "Yes, ma'am, they are."

She wouldn't give the woman the satisfaction of saying she wanted the people gone, as well.

"Have they said how long they intend to stay?"

How was this her business? But that answer would start sparks. "Don't worry. They never stay long. You'll have your view of the ocean back before you know it." Diversion needed now. "We have some new items on the brunch menu you'll want to try. Claire added a heart-healthy sausage and egg strata made with an egg substitute. You'll find it on the buffet."

The woman sniffed. "Are you insinuating I'm at death's door? Don't bury me yet, young lady."

She couldn't win with this woman, no matter what was said. "David mentioned you have some health concerns that brought him home early from an assignment. I only wanted to be helpful."

There. Talk your way out of that one. If she denied the health issues, she would have to admit she'd tricked her son into rushing to her aid for nothing. Starr waited for a three count that certainly felt like a guilty silence to her before the conversational thread picked up again.

"I imagine I'll try your sister's new concoction over

on the buffet. It never hurts to be careful with our diet."
She passed the menu back up to Starr. "Of course I'll
take my regular pot of mint tea."

Hmmm… A crafty dodge if ever she'd heard one.
Not that it mattered because she was staying clear of
David now.

She turned toward the buffet ready to escort her
cranky customer over to load her plate and, ah, no. Starr
flinched. Apparently Ashley had been overwhelmed by
the task of containing the Ciminos. Aunt Essie was busy
making her way from one table to the next passing out
flyers for heaven only knew what. She usually tried to
hock cooking herbs. Weeds she grew in the back of the
mini-hothouse window of her van.

Starr only wished she could split herself in half and
keep Essie Cimino and Alice Hamilton-Reis apart.

Why had she made such an effort to keep the woman
away from the Cimino crowd? It shouldn't matter
anymore if David's mother parked herself on the RV
steps every single day griping. It shouldn't matter at all
what the woman thought…unless Starr cared about
David's world.

Ah, rats. The pencil snapped between her fingers.

She was no more over him now than she'd been when
she'd risked shimmying down the trellis to meet up with
him ten years ago.

David carried a glass of sweet tea out onto the
veranda and wished for something stronger, but he

couldn't afford to water down his guard right now. Not until he had a few less Ciminos in residence.

At least he had his mother settled in with a nurse/companion. His mother had nearly argued herself into a heart attack, but he'd stood his ground. If she had health problems, then he wanted someone on hand to watch out for her. He had a job—and he wasn't a qualified health-care professional.

She hadn't been happy, but once she'd realized he didn't intend to head off to another continent right away, she'd calmed down. He settled in a lounger, tipping back his drink. Beach music from the bar next door tempted him to seek out Starr, say hello, tuck her against his chest and dance with her nice and slow, their bodies fitting against each other.

His gaze scanned the yard, over to the caravan to ensure they were all locked down tight for the night. Only to find instead they were in the midst of a late evening barbecue. They'd rolled out the cabana and a mini charcoal grill with... He caught the scent of hot dogs on the ocean breeze.

Lawn chairs littered the beachy scene. And in the middle stood Starr, silhouetted by a bug candle and a tiki torch.

From her stiff stance and hands on her hips, she didn't appear at all cheerful. Which meant David was far from happy himself. Protectiveness roiled through him. Staying put was not an option.

Setting his glass of tea aside, he surged to his feet.

He took the side stairs two at a time and made his way across the lawn not at a run, but at a determined walk that left deep footsteps in the sandy lawn.

Just as he made it to the first RV, a man stepped from through the door and stopped his progress.

"Whoops. 'Scuse me." Frederick Cimino, Starr's father, swung shut the door, holding a bag of marshmallows. "Hey, you're that neighbor cop kid, aren't you?"

David normally didn't trot out his credentials and he certainly didn't brag, but he absolutely wanted to intimidate the crap out of this man who'd made Starr's childhood a living hell. "Special agent."

"Ah, an agent." Frederick rocked back on his heels, his sandals digging into the sand. "All that money and still you decide to work. Gotta admit, I don't understand that."

"Gives me a reason to wake up in the morning." David kept Starr in his peripheral vision while taking this opportunity to find out more about her father. Knowing the opponent always offered an edge.

Starr's father grinned. "Who says a man needs to wake up early?"

"I imagine it's all about perspective." Exerting some pressure on the man could only benefit and it certainly couldn't do any harm. "From my perspective, you have a great deal of cargo stored in these RVs. I'm sure you have documentation for its purchase, and none of it just fell off the back of some truck."

"Why, Special Agent Man, you're lucky I'm easygoing or I could take offense at that." His eyes might be the same shade of brown as Starr's, but they held none of her giving honesty.

Bad karma for Frederick. David had stood nose to nose with some of the world's worst terrorists. This man *would* leave, sooner or later.

David lounged against the side of the RV, blinked slowly. Mostly to tamp down how much the man pissed him off simply by existing. "I imagine you won't take offense, because I'm not a man you want to anger."

Frederick was smart enough to nod an agreement. "Starr's enough of a Cimino to know a sweet deal when she sees it. So I kind of figured we'd end up family one day. Why would I want to piss you off? We're all about making the most of a good thing."

It was all he could do not to throw the man off the property then and there for talking about Starr, much less occupying the same piece of land. Good God, as if she should sell herself to the highest bidder. David vowed right there, these people would be gone before they had another week to so much as bother Starr.

But for some reason Starr couldn't bring herself to evict these freeloaders, which further emphasized his notion to take her away from here now. With her out of Charleston, he could work with his contacts at the local police department to keep the area safe—and make it clear to the Ciminos that all the security labeled this a no-scam zone.

For tonight, he would have to back off. But the

Ciminos' days here were definitely numbered and he would keep Starr out of their path so they could wreak as little havoc as possible over her psyche in the interim.

He now had a plan, all he had to do was get her to go along with it.

Starr stuffed her head under her pillow, longing to recapture the tingling sensation of her dream.

She and David. Together. Far away from here with no concerns but totally immersing the other in pleasure until they both couldn't contain the building cries of completion.

Instead the only sound she heard was that blasted ringing of the telephone. On and on it went with annoying persistence. She punched either side of the pillow, sealing it around her head until she needed to peek her nose out for air.

The phone rang again. Persistent person, whoever it was.

She flopped over onto her back and reached for the receiver. "It's not even eight o'clock yet, so if you're a telemarketer, I'm going to stick pins in a voodoo doll bearing your image."

"I hear it's your day off."

David's voice rumbled in her ear, rekindling the searing need through her veins coming so close to the explicit coupling in her dreams. She swallowed to clear her throat, and yes, steady her heart rate and breathing before she answered.

"You hear? You must mean you've been bugging my sister.... Let me guess which one." She tapped her temple, sagging back into her pillow and wishing she'd chosen to wear at least a T-shirt to sleep last night.

But it had been so hot and her air conditioner didn't work well, so she'd slept naked with only a sheet that now barely covered her since she'd tangled it around her legs in her restless sleep. "My guess is you went for Ashley since she was probably softened up from that thoughtful gift you gave her."

"Nope. Wrong guess. You lose the prize."

Her hand slid restlessly over her bare stomach, her skin over-sensitized. "If you're the prize then—"

"All right," he interrupted with a low laugh, "no need to get spiteful."

She stroked her fingers over her stomach in a light touch, back and forth, higher every time. "I thought we were bantering."

That stopped him short. His breathing went heavier on the other end of the line. "Bantering, huh?"

She hadn't meant to show her hand that fast. Verbally backtracking, she rushed to speak, her hand stalling just below her breasts. "So Claire sold me out."

"Claire let me know you've worked the past three weeks without a day off."

"That's none of your business."

"You're right. And somehow I managed to find out anyway."

Starr rolled to her side, gathering a pillow against her

chest in counter-pressure against the ache begging for fulfillment. "I imagine that's a great skill in your line of work, prying information out of people."

"Who said I needed to pry it out her? Maybe she thinks you and I have some things to talk about." His voice went low and intimate.

With the tenor of his voice now, just talking could well send her over the edge.

"Just talking? That would be a first for the two of us." Even though simply the sound of his voice turned her on, there was still some truth to the fact that they had spent precious little time conversing.

"Unless you're afraid to be alone with me."

Was she? She hadn't considered a confrontation with him after her realization that this attraction for him wasn't going away after all. But now that she knew that simple truth, maybe it was time to put everything out in the open.

God, this was scarier than she'd expected. It was one thing to think about the fact that she still harbored some kind of unresolved feelings for David. It was quite another to come outright and make herself vulnerable by telling him.

Her gaze strayed to her window, gauzy sheers puffy with gusts from the inefficient air conditioner. The beach stretched with RVs, reminding her of their differences. But she'd grown beyond her upbringing. Right? Made something of herself.

Oddly enough, her parents seemed to be awake unusually early today, as well. Their front door swung open, Frederick stepping out in his jeans shorts and a Grateful Dead T-shirt.

Then he held his hand out to help a woman leave.

David's mother.

Starr shot up straight in her bed. What in the world was she doing there? Gita followed. Starr sagged back against the headboard. Old Alice must be lodging her complaints early these days.

Starr punched her pillow, the air growing chilly without the least help from any decrepit AC.

She measured her words with the same care she put into mixing her paints to achieve just the right hue. "We have a problem that appears to be mutual. We don't want the same things from life, but there's this rogue attraction between us. Since I'm not leaving my house or business, and it seems the Hamilton-Reis Historical Landmark will be there until the end of time, we will be running into each other for years to come. We have to be able to move on with our lives. We can't be sneaking quickies at ninety years old."

That low and sexy laugh of his caressed through the phone lines and over her again. "I bet you'll still be hot as hell."

She couldn't contain her laughter in return, or the arousal their camaraderie brought. She squeezed her legs together against the tender ache and answered, "And you'll still be full of it."

"Don't doubt your appeal."

In that moment she felt the wide chasm of impossibility. "How are we going to put this past us once and for all?"

"That's what you want?"

"Yes," she lied to herself—and to him—again. "Don't you?"

"Of course I want the same thing you do," he answered in that damned evasive way of his that drove her crazy. "Will you trust me and let's try something we've never tried before?"

The possibilities shimmered through her until she couldn't keep her hand from traveling up to cup her breast so heavy and hungry from wanting him. But her own touch wasn't enough. She couldn't evade the truth. She needed him right now at least, consequences be damned.

"Okay. What's your new idea for us try out, David?"

Six

"David, are you going to tell me where we are going before we actually get there?"

Behind the wheel of his Lexus, David kept his eyes on the road, a much safer place to look than at the woman beside him. Soon enough he would have plenty of time to stare at her nonstop.

This outing had taken some fast maneuvering, but he'd come up with a plan he thought would entrance her. He'd also left the house well guarded through his connections at the Charleston Police Department, plus some privately hired guards. He had a good line on a possible debit-card snitching scam the Ciminos may have tried to run in Dallas, Texas, malls.

With luck, he could at least get the cops to arrest them and bring them up on charges. They might well get away with only community service and a fine, but he hoped the threat would be enough to let them know he meant business. Then they would stay the hell away from Charleston in the future.

It had been a near thing getting Starr to leave once they'd seen Frederick Cimino standing out front with his hand painted sign: two for one omelet special. The older man had vowed he'd only wanted to help—and make a little money if they didn't mind sharing a small percentage.

Claire in full fury stomping down the front steps had been enough to scare five Fredericks. Starr had reluctantly left once her father cracked the sign over his knee and made tracks back for the RV beach cabana.

Meanwhile, David could focus his attention on Starr for the next two days. It struck him how they'd spent a large part of their relationship trying to find time alone. Luckily, he had far more resources at his disposal than during his teen years. "Where do you want to go?"

When she didn't answer him, he glanced away from the road over to her sitting in the passenger seat in her low-slung skirt and double tank tops. The noonday sun shone through the window, glinting off the shell necklace that drew his attention to places he could linger for longer than was safe while driving.

She toyed with the larger shell dangling at the

center of the necklace, between her breasts. "Don't you have a plan?"

He dragged his attention back to the highway. "Of course I do, but if you have a preference, I'm always open to suggestion."

"I think for now, I'll see what you have in mind."

Starr giving over control so easily? That was rare. They usually played tug-of-war for a while, but he wouldn't question the victory, although the tussle was sometimes fun. Or rather the making-up had often been mind blowing.

He knew full well odds were strong that they would end up in bed together during these next couple of days. He'd come prepared. But he'd made reservations for two rooms just in case. The choice would be hers. However, once she made it, if she decided on them being together…

Adrenaline pulsed through him at even the thought. "I appreciate your trust. I promise you won't be sorry."

He *would* deliver. And this time, he had something more than sex to offer her—although he hoped they would end up in bed together. Still, in watching her with her relatives, seeing hints of that vulnerable girl she'd once been, he knew he needed to give her something more before he left.

Last year, she'd vowed he'd given her the confidence to open her own business. Having that kind of sway over her life had made his feet itchy then. Even now, a crick started in his neck. However, he knew he wouldn't be free to leave until he gave her one last piece he saw missing in her self-confidence—the strength to say farewell to her relatives for good.

David pulled the car off the main highway onto a two-lane side road, leading to the small privately owned airport.

He'd done further research on Seth Jansen and after a couple of conversations with the man, found him to be a savvy businessman with a keen entrepreneurial eye. Not to mention a helluva gut sense when it came to security. Jansen's airport security inventions had made him a millionaire. His joint search-and-rescue venture with fellow air force pararescueman Rick DeMassi would be a real asset to the community.

David couldn't help but admire a guy who, even after he'd made his millions, still sought ways to give back to the world around him. The privately owned airport sported two hangars, one for Seth's five planes to rent out—a couple of Cessna 152s used for flight training, a Cessna 172, a Cessna 182 and a twin-engine Learjet that he would be using to transport David and Starr.

In the other hangar, he kept his planes for fun—like a World War II Corsair. Jansen had an adventurous spirit, which would work well since David needed the man to be flexible about their plans today.

Starr twisted in her seat, pulling her sunglasses on top of her head as if to see more clearly. She tucked the glasses in place, pulling back her tangle of curls. "An airport? Uh, David, when I said I was up for whatever you had planned, I was thinking more in terms of Italian food versus Mexican food. I wasn't envisioning actually flying to the countries."

He drove the car into the small parking lot, tires crunching on gravel. Shifting the vehicle into park, he turned to face her, staring back at her through his own shades.

"Well, that would be a shame, because travel is exactly what I have in mind."

Starr watched David walk toward the tiny airport terminal while she waited in the running car, air-conditioning humming gently. She'd told him to go on inside without her.

She hadn't told him why.

Fishing in her canvas purse stitched with shells painted to match her necklace, Starr dug out her cell phone. She punched in the numbers for her sister's cell and waited for the pickup.

"Claire," she said without preamble, "I can't believe you told David I could leave for two days. You even went so far as to pack a suitcase for me." She double-checked to make sure David was still inside the terminal—yes—before continuing, "Are you *trying* to get my heart stomped?"

It was one thing to allow herself to spend time with David, talk to him, even sleep with him again. But leave Charleston with him? Be completely and totally alone together in another state? That darn near scared her flip-flops off.

Claire sighed on the other end of the phone with an

older-sister indulgence even though she was only a few years older. "I'm trying to give you a chance to figure out this thing between the two of you once and for all, away from here, away from his mother, your relatives, even this house and your stupid belief that you're not good enough for him."

"I never said that," she replied automatically.

"But you've thought it."

She hadn't bought into that line of garbage, had she?

"But what about my folks? I can't leave you and Ashley to handle all of that."

"What's to handle?" Claire asked with her usual brusque efficiency. "They're here. They eat. Vic's around if I have a concern. Besides, it's you they want to bother, not me."

"But they'll wonder where I went."

"I'll tell them you had a conference related to the business. You left early and you send your regrets, so on and so forth, blah, blah, blah…. What do you think you can do that we can't?"

Starr scrunched her toes into her flip-flops and studied the tiny row of shells painted along the straps. "That's not my point. They're not your responsibility."

"Starr, am I or am I not your sister?"

How could she even ask? "You know you are."

"Damn straight. I am more your relative than any of those people inside those dilapidated homes on wheels. You have done at least this much and more for me in the past. Let me give you a couple of days."

Starr clutched the cell phone, tears stinging her eyes. How had she gotten so lucky to land such an amazing family second go round? "Okay. You're really too generous, but I'll consider it if—and I do mean *if*—David's plans sound like something I can handle."

"Just remember, he's a *man*," Claire drew the word out with wicked intensity, "not a glue gun."

Starr sighed. "Not funny." But a laugh escaped anyway because it was a little funny, and then she sobered. "Promise me you'll keep the cash-register drawer locked tight."

"Sister, I may be generous, but I'm not a fool." Her ever-practical tone brokered no question on that one. "Don't worry."

"But I didn't say for sure that I'm going."

"Yeah, right. See you in a couple of days."

The phone line disconnected.

Starr stared at her silent cell. Was she that transparent? The notion made her want to shout for David and demand that he drive her back to her carriage house pronto. But being contrary wouldn't solve anything.

She had decided to try and work through her residual feelings for him and here was her chance. She just needed to be brave enough to take it. Given all the hardships she'd faced as a child, she was tough. Deep down tough enough to handle anything. She needed to call on that steely spine now to see this through, for both their sakes so she could go of him once and for all…or not?

The airport terminal door swung open. David stepped through, with the Seth at his side. Wow, David really had put some planning into this.

She reached to turn off the car and pulled the keys free. When her feet hit the gravel and she slammed the door shut behind her, David turned toward her, his gaze holding hers for one of those long, electrified seconds that made her remember what it felt like to be a teenager. Then he turned away, said something to Seth that made him nod and head toward the hangar alone.

David started toward her. Lord, he was hotter than the steam rising off the runway. She spent so much time avoiding the attraction, she rarely allowed herself the indulgence of simply looking at him. Today, he appeared so the wealthy Southern male heading for a golf course or on a vacation in his pressed khakis and polo shirt. But those muscles, they still caught her off guard since she'd spent much more time with the leaner teen than the adult male.

His dark hair glinted in the afternoon sun with just a hint of brown in the black. She'd once dreamed of the babies they might have, dark-haired angels with that hint of his devilish smile.

David stopped toe-to-toe with her, not touching. Not needing to. She felt his presence strongly enough.

He adjusted the briefcase he carried in his hand. "I assume this means you've decided to go."

"David, where *are* we going?" she repeated her question from earlier.

"Where do you want to go?" he repeated his same answer, except this time they were nose-to-nose and standing at an airport, so the possibilities were far reaching.

And okay, growing more enticing by the moment.

Except how could he not have a plan? That blew her away. David always had a plan. He was always in charge. He was letting her do the picking?

Her eyebrows pinched together. "Surely you can't mean that. Don't you have to file a flight plan or something?"

He held up the briefcase. "I already have a number of them worked up with Seth for a variety of options. What would you like to see? Shall we go to the lush Louisiana plantations in Natchitoches where we can see the folk-art murals of Clementine Hunter? What about R. C. Gorman's Navajo Gallery in Taos, New Mexico? Or maybe you prefer a trip up New England way to see the work of the eclectic sculptor Joseph Cornell."

How did he know of the assemblage sculptor who combined photographs and bric-a-brac, something so appealing to her own eclectic style? David had certainly done his homework in researching types that would appeal to her. Knowing he'd thought about her that much made her a little breathless.

"What is your point, David?"

"They're all famous self-taught artists."

"That's really thoughtful of you."

He stared at her and waited.

"You want me to make a decision…." And she sensed

something more. Self-taught. "Hey, not so subtle after all. I get it. I should value my art more."

"You said it—" he tapped her on the nose "—not me." He pulled his keys from her hands and thumbed the button to pop the trunk. He pulled out two small suitcases, one she recognized as her own. The things Claire had packed for her.

Hefting the suitcases and his briefcase, David strutted toward the hangar, leaving her to follow whenever she chose.

Lean hips showcased just so in those khaki pants. His polo shirt caressed shoulders so broad and muscular she could rest her hands on them and her fingers would lie flat. He might not need to work but he kept his body and mind honed for his job, a job that offered something of value to society and she couldn't help but admire that.

He made sure little old ladies didn't get scammed by people like her uncle Benny. Fewer mothers lost their diaper bags, forced to file a report while the hungry baby cried.

Sure he dealt on a larger scale, but she thought small scale. Day to day.

She frowned. Was that a holdover from her childhood when she could only think of surviving a day at a time? Something she could address later, because right now it sounded like a plan for the day. She would admire his cute butt and she would go with…

"All right," she shouted after him. "I want to see R. C. Gorman's art gallery."

Without breaking his pace, he held up his briefcase and continued toward the hangar. "Okay then. We'll go to New Mexico."

God, but it had been a tough choice because she would have liked to simply enjoy viewing them all, and she knew if she asked David, he would make that happen. He had always wanted her to do nothing but follow him around the world. And she could see herself enjoying that for a year or even two before she needed home, routine, a normal life he would consider boring.

But for today—or even the next couple of days, she would be the adventurous creature David always encouraged her to be.

And then the possibilities washed over her.

She'd just committed to going away for a weekend with David. Alone, to a hotel, where they would most certainly be doing more than "just talking."

Seven

He had Starr in the Learjet with Seth Jansen piloting them through the bright skies to New Mexico.

Still half-certain he was in the middle of one of his dreams about Starr, David stretched his legs in front of him, watching her stare out the window at the clouds puffing past. The gentle hum of the twin engines afforded them a sense of privacy from Seth flying the craft while they sat in the back of the six-seater.

Finally, he had her alone and away from those blood-sucking leeches she called relatives, thanks to the help of Claire. Her real relative, for that matter. The kind that counted, a person who had Starr's best interest at heart.

Just the two of them together to work through this

off-the-charts attraction that had dogged them through a decade. He couldn't put it off any longer.

Still, questions from home rattled around inside his brain, drowning out the soft buzz of the airplane's twin engines. If only he could figure out why in the hell her family had chosen now to show up. What did they want? Because the Ciminos always wanted something.

At seventeen he'd found Starr bawling her eyes out two days into one of the Ciminos' visits. She'd been terrified of what would disappear from Aunt Libby's house when they left. She'd been afraid that maybe this time she would leave with them to protect those she loved.

Like hell.

Starr rolled her head along her seat to look from her window to him.

"Thank you for planning this. I really haven't gotten away from the restaurant…" She plowed her fingers through those amazing curls, her cheeks puffing with her exhale. "I don't know how long. Probably since we officially opened Beachcombers' doors two years ago."

"It's hard work starting up your own business. You and your sisters have taken on a lot." The clouds broke, revealing the long stretch of desert below. Not much longer and they would be landing.

A smile tugged up her plump lips. "Aunt Libby left us an amazing legacy."

"That piece of land certainly is prime." He'd been approached more times than he could count with buyers for his family's house, but aside from the fact that he couldn't evict his mother, something inside him hesitated to part with the home his family had occupied for over two hundred years.

"I didn't mean the realty or bricks. I meant the concept of home. This was the best way we could think of to keep it." She waved aside the air in front of her. "That's all beside the point. I was thanking you."

"You're welcome." For what, he wasn't sure, not that he intended to admit it.

Her smile returned. "This brings back memories."

"Of?" he prodded.

"Senior prom. Except we're in a plane rather than a limo." She ran her hands over the leather armrests. "Everything's nicer than what I'm used to."

"Is that okay?" He tried to gauge her reaction. He never knew what to expect with Starr. Of course that was part of her allure. He couldn't help but think of that moment on the dock just a couple of days ago when they'd driven each other so crazy he'd nearly forgotten about everything around him.

She scrunched her nose and sank into the luxury of her seat. "I'd be an ungrateful brat if I say no. Besides, only an idiot wants to deal with layovers, security screenings and delays."

"Hey, I like chili dogs better than caviar." He covered her hand with his, his thumb rubbing along the inside of her wrist, as much seduction as he would allow himself for the moment. "It's not always about the money for me."

Her eyebrows rose in apparent surprise. "I'm glad to hear you know that."

He shifted to meet her gaze dead-on, finding it strange they'd never talked about things like this before. But then they'd never had this stretch of time before and it wasn't as if he could touch her the way he wanted while Seth piloted the plane a few feet away.

"The money *does* give me the opportunity to live my life exactly the way I want, Coney dogs in Shea Stadium if I'm in the mood. And not just self-indulgent choices, either. I can make morality choices at work purely based on what I think is right, no concerns about playing politics to get ahead and make a higher pay grade. I'm lucky as hell and I know it."

"And yet you continue to advance anyway."

He stayed silent, savoring the soft skin of her wrist. No need to acknowledge the obvious in her statement.

"This whole day is so surreal, just leaving everything behind." She glanced up at their pilot with the headset on and leaned closer to David. "I appreciate your organizing it for me, but I'm not sure I can guarantee the day is going to end the way I believe you want it to."

She couldn't be any plainer than that, and as much as he wanted her, he wasn't into coercion. She'd been pressured enough in her lifetime as a kid.

The trained investigator in him could see the residual impacts of her upbringing in her. The way she always expected someone to want something from her in exchange. Why hadn't he noticed that before?

Because he'd been too busy thinking with the other head, damn it. Something he needed to rectify now, even when the heat between them continued to flare.

"This is a no-strings offer. We're going to land, have a quick late lunch on our way to the gallery and then look at some artwork before supper. If after supper, you want to go straight to your room alone, that's your call." He meant it, no matter how much he wanted to be with her, it would be mutual or not at all. "We have enough history between us for you to know that I would never hold you to something unless you want the same thing."

She stared back into his eyes, holding for a long drone of the engines before finally nodding. "I trust you."

"Good. Good."

He was glad she did because staying strong against the temptation while sleeping in the room next to Starr would be total torture. All advances in the work world aside, he wasn't so sure he'd made the wisest move in his personal life.

Still questioning his own relationship IQ two hours after landing in New Mexico, David watched Starr's face as she strolled slowly through the gallery.

She wove around the sparse remaining tourists still hanging around in the final minutes before closing. He took note of even the slightest hesitation, searching for preferences of ceramics over silkscreens. Or paper casts over landscapes. She seemed taken in by *all* of it…studying the swirls and colors of each piece.

Finally she paused by a ceramic plate with a silly-looking orange cat on it. Seemed a rather odd choice to him, but then art was in the eye of the beholder and all that. This was her gig. "Do you want it?"

"No." She blinked fast as if pulled from a trance and glanced back over her shoulder at him. "No! Don't even go there, Agent Money Bags. Do not, under any circumstances, buy that for me. You're going to make it impossible for me to enjoy this if I have to worry about admiring any other pieces of artwork for fear you'll whip out your credit card."

"You could throw a 'thanks anyway' in there somewhere." He felt compelled to add. He had just offered to chunk out some serious cash for a tabby-cat plate.

"Your ego doesn't need it." She turned her back to him and returned to studying the array of artwork on the walls and in display cabinets.

"You're right." He closed the few feet between them until he was standing directly behind her. He kept his hands in his pockets even though he wanted to reach for her and pull her so she leaned back against him. He'd sworn there were no strings until she gave an indication otherwise and he was a man of his word. "Good thing I have you around to help me keep my ego in check."

"Yeah, well, since your ego's been deflated for the day, I guess I can give you that thanks for the thought—although I only hesitated because it reminded me of a pet I had for two weeks once when I was eight." She glanced over her shoulder at him; a whimsical smile lighting her brown eyes that shared the same color as her father, but none of the same sentiment, hers so sincere. "And thank you for the whole day. Seeing these in books is nothing like seeing them for real."

"There are two more artists on my short list. With just a simple call to your sister, we could extend the trip and see the works of both." He edged closer, hands still in his pockets, not that it helped *him* any. He could feel the heat of her radiating through the scant few inches between them. Nothing overt that any of the three people remaining in the gallery would see, but God, he couldn't miss it. "You should see the artists I put on my long list."

She licked her lips as if thirsty—heaven help them both if she kept that up much longer. "What about your mother's health concerns?"

"I've hired a nurse to stay at the house and keep watch over her. I couldn't hang there 24/7, and I'm not a health-care professional anyway. A live-in seemed the best solution."

"But you check with the nurse, of course."

"Of course," he repeated. He was a detail man and right now, nothing was more important to him than putting his situation with Starr to rest so he—and the Caravan gang—didn't hurt her again.

"What does the nurse have to say?" Starr's attention shuffled to a series of landscapes with a woman and flowers.

"You're actually worried about my mother even after

the way she's treated you all these years?" All the more reason to make sure he read the signs correctly with Starr and treated her right. He flattened his hands over hers on the glass of the display case, so cool after the heat of the desert sun.

"Yes, I worry about her. She's your mother. If she's deeply ill, I would hate to take you away from her bedside at a critical time, although, um, she looked healthy at brunch last week."

He had to agree that his mother seemed fine, which was a good thing. He suspected she'd wanted attention and things would settle down now. "Other than a slightly elevated blood pressure, she's actually healthy as a horse. I suspect she just gets lonely sometimes and feels the need to call me home."

"It would help if you had siblings. I don't know what I would do without my sisters to help me." Her eyes took on a dreamy look as she stared at the desert landscape of a woman at the waterside.

"They're lucky to have you, too." He finally let himself touch her again, just a hand on her shoulder, a simple, platonic-like squeeze. "Don't sell yourself short."

"Thank you, and I don't."

He kept his hand light on her shoulder, nothing sexual. Problem was his thoughts were anything but platonic. His imagination went into overdrive envisioning what he would do if they were alone in this position.

First, he would flatten his hand to the wall by her head and wrap his arm around her waist, lifting her, pulling her against him. Just a simple adjustment of their bodies and he would be able to slide inside her. Somehow his thoughts created a tangible heat of a full-body press swelling between them until he could almost swear she felt it, too.

Starr shuffled from foot to foot until she made it back to her cat plate again.

David kept his hand on her shoulder through the move. "So do you like that piece because it reminds you of your old pet?"

"Yes." Her answer slid from her lips a bit breathier than before. She paused, cleared her throat and continued, "I like it so much I want to leave it right here for other people to enjoy, too."

He gripped both her biceps and turned her around to face him, hands still cupping her upper arms. "Damn, you're good."

She swayed toward him, pupils widening in her dark eyes with a deep desire he absolutely couldn't misread. "And you're so very bad."

"Which is what makes us so incredible together."

"Ah, David," she whispered, his name drawn out on a sigh, a plea he'd heard often enough in the past to know what she wanted. "I thought I told you I couldn't promise this would end with us in bed."

She startled as a college-aged man walked by pushing a broom. The place was closing and time was nearing to head to the hotel for the night. If they actually made it to the hotel…

Thank goodness he'd made a plan for them to have a romantic getaway, just in case she changed her mind about the no-sex rule. It seemed his preparations would be implemented in mind-blowing, fulfilling detail very soon.

But first, he planned to draw out the pleasure with a tantalizing wait.

David dipped his head, his mouth near her ear. "I know what you said and I agreed things would only be mutual. And I would bet every last one of my training instincts that what I'm feeling right now is very mutual and you've decided it's fruitless to resist."

Eight

"Drive faster," Starr urged from her passenger seat in the Mercedes convertible rental, car top down.

Where had David made their hotel reservations? The next state over?

"You want me to speed up? No can do, babe. I'm already pegged on the limit and that whole law-enforcement official thing obligates me to follow the rules of the road."

He kept a steady pace with cruise control. The car lights beamed ahead, luminescent strips on the asphalt the only glow on the deserted back highway.

Again he delayed fulfilling her need for him, which left her fidgeting in her seat as she had all through dinner. The wind spirited into the neck of his polo shirt just the way her hands longed to do.

They'd been driving for at least forty-five minutes since they'd left the five-star restaurant he'd chosen for their supper. He'd even selected an establishment much like Beachcombers so she could gather work ideas about food—although he'd surprised her when he'd told her they wouldn't be staying there for the night.

Not that she'd been able to think about work or even sleeping. All she'd been able to contemplate during the interminable meal was getting him alone and naked.

Still, he'd drawn out the pleasure, making each bite an aphrodisiac moment. He'd been seductive from the start in everything he'd chosen in this outing. This man in full-tilt charmer mode was irresistible.

She tore her gaze away from him. Her eyes took in the endless stretch of rocky desert on either side of the highway. Nothing but telephone poles, scattered cacti and the occasional Joshua tree, the dry air so different from the humid beach climate she'd come to love at Aunt Libby's.

The gritty wind tore at her hair with a wild abandon that fit the moment, tugging at the scarf he'd brought along to tie back her curls. Eventually she whipped the silky length free and let the wind have its way with her locks much the way she'd given over control of this evening to David.

He obviously had somewhere out of the way in mind, which meant a long time for them to simmer in the car.

Might as well make the best use of this time. She had memories to store.

She slid her hand across the seat, teasing up the length of his thigh, enjoying the heat and ripple of muscle under the rough texture of khaki. "And there's nothing I could do to entice you to take a shortcut?"

Grinning, she squeezed his leg, high, just shy of his fly.

David clamped a hand around her wrist. "Much more of that and we'll end up in a ditch."

He had a point. She sagged back against her seat, resolved to wait.

Except then he turned off the road.

"David? Where's the hotel?" She didn't see any signs of civilization even on the horizon.

"Who said anything about a hotel yet?"

The smile returned to her lips and swirled around inside her, as well. No more waiting, and she did so approve of his plan. She'd always enjoyed the times they'd made love outside as opposed to times they'd sneaked around in his room or hers. Outside seemed so much more neutral. Not her world or his.

He shut off the engine then turned the key to keep the music going, low classical tunes to suit the romance of the moment. Reaching behind the seat, he tugged free an Aztec blanket that would undoubtedly ward off the chill of the desert night because yes, yes, yes she could see in his eyes that soon they would be shedding at least some of their clothes.

She hooked her finger in the neck of his shirt. "How

about you come over here so we don't have to deal with the steering wheel."

"Yes, ma'am." He cupped her waist and hefted her up, sliding into her seat as he settled her onto his lap.

David tugged the blanket around her, tenting it over their shoulders, their bodies already starting a furnace of heat inside. The dashboard lights shone along with the full yellow moon to cast shadows over his square jaw clenched in restraint as a lonely coyote howled in the distance. The breadth of his shoulders alone stole the air from her lungs, and yet this strong man had set her onto his lap with such gentle ease, held her now in such careful, seductive hands.

What a rush.

Her starving hands tugged his polo shirt free of his pants, whipping it over his head and onto the steering wheel.

He chuckled low. "I've always liked how you know what you want."

"You taught me to take what I need."

He growled his appreciation of her words, his hands making slow and tantalizing work of peeling each of her tank tops off, touching her, caressing her, teasing her until they rubbed chest to chest. "Feel free then to act on that now to your heart's content."

Heart? The word made her uncomfortable, so she focused instead on the heavy thudding of his heart under her hand and dipped to press her lips to the warmth of his skin, covering the pulse increasing by the second.

She nibbled along his shoulder, the salty taste of him sending an erotic surge through her. "We've done it in a sandy region before, but this is a bit different."

He nipped her ear. "I thought you might enjoy the wild abandon of the desert."

"The solitude, as well. Just the two of us." She slid her arms around his back, holding him, holding on to this moment as tightly. "No parents on either side of the property line."

No different goals and backgrounds dividing them just as tangibly.

"A definite plus."

The richness of the experience was only enhanced because of the richness of their day together, the fun of touring the gallery. She knew he'd only gone there for her and would probably have preferred one of those Coney dogs and a ball game, but that he'd found something to enjoy in her world, well, that turned her inside out.

And totally *turned* her on.

He traced along the edge of her ear, soothing the nip, his breath hot along with his words and the stroke of his hands. "I also liked the notion that the stars are so vibrant."

"I guess I never thought about that when we traveled this way when I was a kid."

"Whenever I come this way on business, it makes me think of you, because of all the times we made out on the beach."

"You said the constellations reminded you of my name."

"I was such a sap back then." He sagged back, shaking his head with a low rumble of laughter.

"Sappy's not so bad if you want to get a girl into bed." She cupped his face in her hands, her thumbs retracing the strong cut of his cheekbones.

"I got you here today."

"Maybe *I* got *you*." She rubbed her over-sensitized breasts against his chest.

"Damn, you make me hot. You were a handful as a teenager and you're all that and more now."

"Is that a compliment?"

His hands slid up between them to shape around her breasts, rubbing, tempting with just the right amount of pressure. "What do you think?"

How could being with him feel so wonderfully right for her and yet be wrong at the same time? He'd done this thoughtful thing in taking her to see the art display, and she'd enjoyed the time away from Beachcombers more than she'd expected. But to her, it was a vacation. She didn't want to live her life this way and David didn't want to live his life in one spot. A fundamental problem they'd never been able to overcome.

Yet the taste he'd given her today of travel had truly shown her how much she would be throwing away. My, how he tempted her. Always had.

Her hands skimmed over his body as if forming over a sculpture. She hadn't done much in that art form, but it was one that had always fascinated her. She would have enjoyed capturing him in clay, her hands recreating from memory the cut and feel of him. Except this was a new feel, this man she'd only had brief contact with a year ago.

She had to be honest with herself; she wanted more. More time. More of him. His chest in particular fascinated her. This adult man was all the more intriguing than the teenage boy she'd been with before. The hard sinew of honed muscles called to her fingers to explore.

They'd taken their time learning about each other's bodies before, out of curiosity, as well as passion. Now the same feelings tingled through her. Did the same things still turn him inside out?

There was only one way to find out.

Starr arched up, traced his strong jawline and pressed her mouth to his. Without hesitation, she opened to him and yes, he swept her mouth with his tongue in bold possession. But she could take, as well as be taken. She sucked with a gentle seduction that all too quickly had another yes rumbling in his chest, his hips rocking under hers. The steely pressure of his erection throbbing between them—even through their clothes—leaving her with no question of how quickly she could tempt him into total arousal. And she'd barely even begun.

He made short work of hiking up her skirt and skimming away her underwear—he'd always been adept at that—before sliding his hands to cup her buttocks, and holy cow there went her blood pressure. David ducked his head to her breast, sucking, drawing on her nipple, his kiss, even the gentle tug of his teeth on her tightened bud with an extra friction that threatened to drive her over the edge from just this one pleasure alone. Then he switched his attention to her other breast while sliding his hand to cup the breast he'd just abandoned, rubbing, plucking.

Her brain went on stun and she lost the ability to think altogether until she felt cool air over her heated flesh and realized he was working the rest of her clothes down and off. She helped wriggle them free while opening his pants.

Arching up, he reached for his wallet perched cleverly within reach on the dashboard and withdrew a small packet. *Condom.* Thank goodness he'd thought of it since she could barely remember her own name, much less how to supply birth control.

A memory flashed through of how they'd learned to use them together. In fact, he'd found great pleasure in letting her…

She took the condom from him and flipped it between her fingers. He stared back at her with his best wicked albeit indulgent—darn him—smile. She straddled his lap, giving as good as she got in the wicked-smile department. She wrapped her hand around him at the base and held on with a strong but tender grip. Letting her smile broaden, she swept her thumb up and down ever so slightly to caress him in the way she remembered he liked. He throbbed in her hand.

Her body pulsed in response. No more waiting. She fit the condom on over him.

He gripped her hips in a firm but gentle hold and lifted her. Sighing, she braced her hands on his shoulders and threw back her head. Ready. Oh, so ready. Still he drew out the moment until she finally realized what he wanted from her. She'd closed her eyes.

She opened them and stared at him, moonlight shimmering overhead and glinting off his clenched jaw. The restraint cost him as much as it did her.

"Now," she panted.

As soon as the word slipped past her lips, he surged upward, into her with a thick and wonderful familiarity that brought tears to her eyes.

"You okay?" he asked, not moving, so deep inside her she vowed she would feel him forever.

She could only nod.

He took her mouth and withdrew, slowly, then filling her, again and again as she reclaimed their skin-tingling rhythm. She lost herself in his strokes, in his kiss with his tongue that thrust in a matching boldness of his body. She clung to him, writhed against him, wrung as much from the moment as she could and tried to ignore the voice inside her insisting she ought to snitch as much from the moment because she feared there wouldn't be another.

Hadn't that always been how they loved? As if living for the last time. They didn't know any other way.

She continued to grip—even claw—at him, at fate, at her own inability to figure out a way to have more with this man than stolen moments. She felt even more the gypsy child filching what she could for herself because there was no one to look out for her.

Except she had this strong and amazing man in her arms. A man who'd thrown her life and emotions into chaos for years. She pulled her mouth from his and scattered kisses along his jaw before burying her face in the crook of his neck and surrendering to sensations.

She knew she spoke, but couldn't pull rational thought together enough to decipher her own rambling litany of want, much less understand his. But oh, she heard the strength of his desire in the tenor of his tone. Knowing she moved him as much as he touched her pitched her forward, over the edge of desire.

Her back arched with the strength of her release, and the sparkling lights above could have been the sky in a nighttime rainbow above or behind her lids in a palate of color. She wasn't sure and couldn't think of anything except the power of the pleasure pulsing through her. He gave her so much and she could do nothing but collapse against him, exhausted.

His rumbling groan of completion vibrated against her skin, jarring a second, echoing release from her sated body.

If only they could stay right here for the rest of the night, wrapped up in a simple Aztec blanket, under the desert's stars.

Tugging the eight ka-jillion thread count Egyptian cotton sheet around her naked body in David's hotel bed, Starr couldn't help but be glad they'd made love in the desert that first time, in the more neutral outdoors.

This high-class hotel with its expensive linens and hop-to bellmen only served to remind her of the chasm between her upbringing and his. She so didn't want to travel down that road of thinking, but couldn't seem to recapture an emotional detour to match the real one they'd taken earlier.

She gave up trying to get comfortable in the unfamiliar surroundings of crystal chandeliers and monochromatic creamy colors and sat, clutching her knees to her chest. "I'm sorry you had to pay for a suite of rooms when we're only going to use one bed."

"The money doesn't matter."

He rolled to his side, tugging a lock of her hair and looking supremely at ease in the monstrous wooden sleigh bed. A huge bouquet of imported tulips and lilies lurked behind him on the nightstand, filling the room with an elegant fragrance that struck her as all wrong for the desert climate outside.

"Money always matters." She yanked the sheet more securely over her breasts. She could get used to the sheets, though. They were truly heavenly. "It shouldn't be squandered."

"Consider that it helped someone meet their bills then. If you're really feeling guilty, then we can just be sure to make love in both beds."

"Oh, and both showers, too." She liked how he thought, the wicked, wonderful man.

"Now you're getting the right idea." He tunneled a hand under the covers to cup her hip, stroking gently, distracting her ever so slightly. "Let's not forget the sofa and there's all this carpet that needs breaking in, as well."

"You *are* an indulgent man. I'll bet you actually eat things from the minibar."

"Is that a trick question?"

She flopped back with an exasperated *argh*. "You are so totally from another universe." She tugged on his arm. "The minibar is always full of way overpriced stuff someone like me can't afford."

"Tonight you can." He swung his feet to the floor, a gust of cool air slithering under the sheets. "What would you like? Some twenty-dollar M&M's?"

"Okay, it's not that bad," she huffed. He didn't have to poke fun at her.

"Really?" His back to her, he continued to speak, irking her all the more with his lack of understanding. "I could have sworn…"

Or maybe he did understand. "Now you're just teasing me."

He turned back around, candy bag in hand and open. He upended it, pouring M&M's all over her torso.

"David!" she squealed.

How like David to ply her with M&M's rather than the champagne in the silver bucket beside the bed. And how wise of him to know this would tickle her funny bone and fancy far more. The thought of common ground intimidated her even as it held obvious appeal. What if he made steps to close the gap between them?

He straddled her. "Did I mention I like twenty-dollar M&M's eaten off a naked woman even more than Coney dogs in Shea Stadium?"

David dipped his head and found a piece of candy nestled in her belly button. He crunched on a couple more, popping some into her mouth, as well, while he feasted, before he rolled to the side, laughing along with her. Once her laughter faded, he gathered her close and oh, where had the tension gone? God, he was good at maneuvering her.

"So money was tight for you growing up," he said with a no-so-subtle probing intensity.

Really good at maneuvering.

"Not tight, so much as always the focus of every action they made." She traced swirls of hair on his chest. "And of course things were tight at Aunt Libby's because she always took in as many girls as she could possibly afford."

"You showed up when you were ten, right?"

"Yes," she slugged his arm. "You know that's right since I've told you before. You never get facts wrong. If you want to know something, just ask me." Although she had to be honest with herself that he had asked her in the past and she'd dodged his questions. She'd become good at that, manufacturing a history for schoolmates that wasn't humiliating.

"Okay, I confess, I'm curious about what brought

you to Charleston." He trailed his fingers along her side, down to her hip and up again to the curve of her breast. "I want to know more about you, something I should have asked when I was seventeen but I was too horny back then to think of anything but getting you naked."

"Yet, here I am naked now, too."

"I still want to get you naked, but I also want to know what happened to bring you here."

There was no mistaking the intensity in those beautiful blue eyes of his eyes she'd once dreamed of seeing in a baby boy they'd made together—silly teenage dreams. Starr tugged herself back to the present and dealing with how much of her past to share. She'd told him precious little as a teen, embarrassed by her parents' shady dealings.

Now, she figured it was probably best not to tell David the total story about how she'd ended up at Aunt Libby's or he might do damage to her family out on the lawn and end his illustrious career with the OSI. His imagination from years on the job could likely hazard a close enough guess.

Instead, she opted to share her early years with Aunt Libby. "The first few months were pretty rocky. I was certain she would boot me out, so I preferred to leave on my own terms. A week after I arrived—" once her ten-year-old self had recovered from her near miss with heat exhaustion in her parents' RV "—I stole a piece of her mother's silver flatware and hid it under my mattress."

He yanked a curl in gentle chastisement. "Sticky little fingers you had, huh?"

"It wasn't my first time. You should probably know I was picking pockets by my fifth birthday. Aunt Libby found it before lunchtime. Looking back, she'd probably dealt with far worse from other girls in the past. But anyhow, I thought for sure I was toast. Instead, I lost recreation time outside and had to polish all her silver."

"She sounds like a savvy lady."

"It took me a few months of pranks to realize she planned to keep me around for as long as I needed her, but I wasn't going to get away with jack."

"I wish I'd spent more time with her."

Starr could feel the automatic retreat inside herself. Her gaze skittered away from his and she plucked at the sheet draped over her. "She wasn't on your mother's bridge-club list."

"That shouldn't have mattered." He rolled her to face him, his eyes holding hers. "And actually works in her favor."

"Whatever." Starr shrugged dismissively, unable to stop old defense patterns from creeping over her. "I kept pushing the boundaries until this one day when I really started to get scared because I liked it here with the sisters and the food."

The admission slipped free in spite of her defenses screaming at her to hold back, not to give away anything someone could use against her later. "And oh, God, how it felt to have a mother figure who fed me and cared how I did in school. Having good stuff in your life means you have something to lose." She swallowed down the lump of anxiety in her throat that still lingered even today. "So I broke her porcelain jewelry box."

"I take it you weren't normally a clumsy child."

Starr nodded. "I was usually very careful not to upset the grown-ups. Aunt Libby went real quiet as she scooped up the pieces. She wouldn't look at me or even scold me. She just left the room." That choking lump grew to tangerine size in her throat. "One of the really bitchy foster girls told me the box had been given to her by her fiancé who died in the Korean War."

"Ah, hell." He gathered her close for a hug, stroking her hair. "You had no way of knowing."

"I heard her cry." She stifled her own sniffle against his chest.

"Nearly seventeen years later and you still feel guilty." He tipped her chin so she could see him. "Babe, I make my living off knowing when people are guilty and when they're not. I'm telling you, you've got to cut yourself some slack or you're never going to get those people out of your backyard."

Her spine straightened and she shrugged free of his grip that urged her to see things in a new and uncomfortable light. "Could you ease off your high horse for just one minute and let me have my crappy-ass memory? I'm trying to share something with you, you thickheaded man. It just takes women more words to get there."

"Fair enough. I'm an interrogator. I should know better." Sitting up, he scooped her up in his lap as if she weighed less than a poodle. "Talk away."

Not exactly the sensitive acknowledgment of her individuality she was looking for…but close. And he smelled good and felt good and who really wanted perfect anyway? Perfect sounded boring.

"I gathered up all my money—none of it stolen because she'd broken me of that habit by then—and I bought a paint set, which pretty much depleted my funds so I couldn't afford a porcelain anything. I got a buddy of mine to build a wooden box with a leather thong latch and I painted it."

She sighed long and hard, remembering the feel and smell of those paints along with the rush of bringing the image in her mind to life…. "Man, did I paint it with a view of the ocean sunrise that blended realism and romanticism until… David, it was really beautiful. It may not have been the box she had but I found I had a talent, something special for just me." She smiled at the memory. "Aunt Libby and I cried together over that box. Then we laughed and celebrated. I had a talent, something that set me apart from all the other girls. Aunt Libby had a way of helping each of us find that something special about ourselves."

She relaxed into his chest as they sat leaning back against the sleigh-bed headboard with her draped across his lap—too comfortable. Too easy to stay this way. "I'm not sure I can fully express to someone like you how much that meant to us, finding out we were special."

"To someone like me?" He went still against her, his voice rumbling under her ear.

Oops. She'd stepped in it, but there was no back-tracking. "Someone born knowing his place in the world. Someone valued from birth. Someone encouraged to stand out…" She shook her head again, embarrassed, wary in a way she hadn't felt in a long time. Putting her whole self out there got tougher rather than easier with age.

He caressed the back of her neck in a gentle massage. "Don't stop there."

Apparently even if she'd stepped in it, he wanted her to keep on wading through. She swallowed down that darned persistent lump. "Why, Special Agent, that was positively sensitive of you, urging me to continue with this emotional discussion."

"I work to understand people for a living. It strikes me that understanding you should have been my number-one priority and yet I worked like hell to…"

"Keep your distance while getting me naked?"

He didn't answer, simply rested his chin on top of her head. An affirmation of sorts.

"So I'll talk." Because if she ever wanted to figure this thing out between her and David, they would have to stop hiding from each other. She wasn't sure where this would lead—to more closeness or the final heartbreak—but this time, they would have to see it through. "Most of us came from situations where it was best not to be noticed. I had problems in my childhood, no question, but David, some of the things I heard from the other girls would break even your hard heart."

"Ashley."

"For one." She thought of so many others, ones who'd found homes, ones who'd gone to mended homes, ones who'd been forced to return home, even though nothing was fixed at all....

Starr blinked back the gritty craziness of the world and focused on what she could repair. "We couldn't exactly take out a hit on Ashley's heartless birth parents who gave her up rather than take on the cost and stress of dealing with her birth defects, but we've given her a family, a home, and we hocked ourselves up to our ears to give her the college education so she could achieve more."

"The education both of you wanted."

She shrugged, not ready to admit that yet, because heaven forbid Ashley should somehow even catch a whiff of the feeling radiating off Starr.

"Babe, you may be right that they could put a dent in my hardened heart." David swept her off his lap and onto her back beside him. "But right now, you're the one chipping away at that pounding rock in the middle of my chest."

Staring up at David looming over her, Starr wondered if she would be able to deny this man anything he asked of her right now.

Nine

David twined his fingers through Starr's hair and watched her sleep, in no real hurry to wake her and launch the morning. The day would start soon enough and he would resume his campaign to persuade her that following him around the world wasn't such a hardship after all. Convincing her wasn't going to be as easy as he'd led himself to believe setting out on this trip.

He thumbed the off button on his cell phone and rested it on the bedside table by the remains of their midnight feast. Thank God the call hadn't woken her because as far as he was concerned she didn't need to know.

Her mother had been picked up by local cops, questioned and ultimately released. There was a chance she was involved in a purse snatching, but Gita had spun the attempt to make it sound as if she was only trying to catch the real thief and—lo and behold—she caught him so she had the woman's stolen purse, which she turned over.

She'd waltzed out of the station on lack of evidence.

Already Starr carried such a chip on her shoulder. Hell, call it what it was—an inferiority complex. Damn. He just didn't get it, because she was the smartest, sharpest, most amazing woman he'd ever laid eyes on. Convincing her, however, helping her overcome the hell of her childhood and find an inherent new sense of self… He still had some work to accomplish in that arena.

He refused to doubt that he could win. But for now, he allowed himself a window of time to forget about the fact they had past problems or a future to settle.

The desert sunrise shone through the hotel skylights, glinting off her skin, reminding him of how he'd worshiped every inch of her through the night. Being with her that first time in the desert had been mind blowing, and damn near control shattering since he hadn't been with anyone else in the past year since he'd last left her.

Something he hadn't told her. Of course they always played these little games with each other, holding back pieces of themselves.

It didn't escape him that she still hadn't told him what had brought her next door to Libby Sullivan's doorstep. Starr was efficient at dodging questions, far better than anyone he'd ever encountered, and he'd interrogated the best. Of course, he didn't want her to feel threatened.

Still he couldn't escape the driving need to know more about her. And what better time than now to gather up as much info about her as possible to use in his quest to win her over? Winning her to his side grew more important the more time he spent with her.

Being with her—well, damn it all—he'd been deluding himself that a couple of days would be enough. So he needed to come up with a way to sway her into taking more time off from that business she loved so much. Why couldn't she see it was just a house? Bricks and wood and nails.

He'd hoped that the excitement of making love out in the open would give her a taste of what was out there to be experienced—beyond the limiting boundaries of home.

Starr sighed and stirred beside him, stretching. He slowed his strokes through her wildly tangled mass of hair, letting her find her own pace waking. Besides, he couldn't deny himself the pleasure of watching her. They'd woken together very few times, only last year the one weekend they'd spent together. While they'd slept together as teens, they'd never been able to share a night.

She kicked the covers, inching her feet free, curling her toes until a subtle *crack, crack, crack* echoed in the otherwise silent room. Turning from his side, she stretched, clutching the sheet to her chest—damn shame—and rolled onto her back, tucking her head into the pillow, her neck arching. Okay, only a saint could hold strong against this enticing goddess greeting the morning.

"Good morning, babe." He kissed the crook of her neck, the first of her erogenous zones he'd discovered in making out with Starr.

"Mmmmm," she answered with a groggy groan, reaching to stroke his chest while tipping her head to give him better access to her neck.

He definitely liked mornings with Starr. Sliding a leg over hers, he trapped her still and trekked toward her breasts. She fidgeted under his touch.

"Morning." She pressed a quick kiss to his shoulder and slid from beneath him. She rolled to her feet, gloriously naked. "Teeth. Gross. Gotta brush them."

From her brusque tone, apparently she wasn't much of a morning person. He grinned at the bit of knowledge and filed it away in his mind as she disappeared into the bathroom. David stuffed a second pillow behind his head and sat up, resting back against the headboard, staring at her stroll back to bed. She crawled across the sheets to rejoin him, pressing a proper good-morning kiss to his mouth before settling in beside him.

"How about room service, or do you want to compare their buffet to your own?"

"If I'm going to call this a true vacation, I guess I should forego the buffet in lieu of room service."

"That's my girl." He nuzzled her neck again before reaching for the phone and placing their order. He considered resuming their lovemaking, but didn't particularly want to be interrupted by room service. "You know, babe, as much as I'm enjoying this, I really don't want to stop halfway through to answer the door for your eggs Benedict."

"So we'll ignore it and order more."

As her hand made its way up his leg, he considered her proposition, seriously contemplated it, but then he remembered last night and how pleasure delayed was pleasure doubled. What better time to advance his goal of learning more about her?

David clamped a hand around her wrist with an inch to spare before she would have been hands on the target and able to talk him into ignoring food through the whole day. "Not yet. Soon though, and I'll make the wait well worth your while."

Starr eased away, studying him through narrowed eyes, crossing her arms over her perfect breasts. Her bottom lip jutted out in an honest to Pete pout. He couldn't stop his grin.

She grabbed a pillow and swatted him. "It's really un-gentlemanly of you to revel in my pain."

"Your pain? You're actually hurting you want me so much?"

As he ducked the next swat of her lethal pillow, he couldn't stop the full-out smile that spread over his face. Call him a knuckle-dragger, but he liked that he had sway over this woman. Heaven knew she pulled him inside out with a look, a touch, a simple wish for a damn cat plate because he knew she still longed for a pet.

He let her rain her downy swats at him for another

couple of swings before looping his arms around her waist and pinning her to the mattress. Tickling. Laughing. And oh, yeah, kissing.

David eased his mouth from hers and brushed a kiss against her ear. "You've had the power to knock me on my ass since the first day I saw you."

She stilled under him. "You seem so self-confident. I didn't think anyone rocked you."

How could she not know? Of course he'd done his best not to let her into his head. Which brought him back around to his wish to crawl inside her brain. As much as he balked at ponying up facts about his life, sharing a piece of himself only seemed fair for what he expected from her. And it was a good interrogation technique. Right?

Whatever you need to tell yourself to get through the day, pal.

He twined one of her curls around his finger. "Actually, there was one other woman who could put the fear of God in me."

"Your mom?"

Staying silent, he shook his head. "Your aunt Libby."

"Why would she do that?"

The luxury sheet started to itch against his bare flesh. "Because she knew what we were doing."

"Aunt Libby *knew?*" She shoved him off her as if somehow the woman could see them now. Starr inched up higher against the headboard, sheet gripped to her breasts. "She knew I was crawling up into your room?"

How the woman had managed to mother anywhere from eight to eighteen children at once he would never know, but his admiration for her ran deeper than the dark Atlantic off Charleston. "She sure did, babe."

"Why didn't she talk to me?"

"Because you're as immovable as a tree stump."

"Why, thank you. I do believe that's the most romantic thing a man's ever said to me. How can I ever resist climbing onto your private jet for another getaway to an exotic locale?"

He considered apologizing for the statement and then figured he might as well opt for the truth. A relationship built on lies to make the other feel better wasn't worth a crap. "You grew up with bullshit flattery and downright lies. I figured you were a woman who would respect the God's honest truth."

She skimmed a finger along his collarbone in an innocent touch that shouldn't have had so much arousing power over him, but it did. He gripped her hand and brought it to his mouth, kissing her palm, more to give himself some distance, control over the situation.

A knock sounded at the door.

He pressed a final kiss to her wrist. "Stay put. I'll get it."

Rolling from the bed to his feet, he grabbed a pair of pajama bottoms from his suitcase and yanked them on before heading out to the sitting area. She was tougher to win over than he'd expected. But then when had anything ever gone the way he'd expected or wanted with Starr? Damn it, he wasn't a quitter. He'd vowed to make the most of these couple of days together and he would push it to the wall on all levels, if that was what it took. Even if it meant doing something far more difficult than staging impromptu cross-country trips. He would do that thing chicks seemed to want most—share feelings.

He shuddered even though there wasn't an air conditioner or fan in sight.

Starr slathered raspberry preserves on her whole-wheat toast, studying David across the small table the entire time. What was he up to now? She could see the wheels turning in his handsome head, although he'd been nothing but charming from the moment they'd sat at the romantic little table with its wrought-iron legs and seat backs shaped like hearts.

Adjusting a button on the pajama top she wore—his pajama top—she figured she would have to look into purchasing a table like this for Beachcombers…. But hadn't he done this a ka-zillion times? Chosen something in their outing that would speak to her and her life?

What about him? What did he want from these couple of days away? Besides the obvious naked time.

She swallowed down her toast with a swig of orange juice. "Okay, so back to the Aunt Libby discussion. I'm stubborn and sometimes I'm so focused on my goal I don't have time to weigh in other people's plans and opinions."

He nodded that blue-blooded regal head of his. "And

I have my own strong opinions. But when it came to you, your aunt Libby knew I had a…"

She'd never seen him wrestle for a word before. Did he not know? Or did he not want to own up? The possibility shimmered through her veins like the glitter spread out on her table in her studio.

"I could be less inflexible when it came to you, and that old lady knew it. She stood nose to nose with me."

Had he just admitted to vulnerability? He had. *Ohmigod.*

Starr set down her juice. His memory must be faulty, although Aunt Libby had had a larger than life quality. "She was a full foot shorter than you. How could she stand nose to nose?"

"Libby Sullivan was a savvy lady." He refilled his coffee, adding nothing else to the steaming cup of java. "She knew how to set the stage for her interrogation and made sure she stood a few porch steps up, on her turf, not mine."

"Did she threaten to tell your mother?" Obviously she hadn't, though, since his mother hadn't found out until prom night. The beautiful evening had been tainted by his mother's sniffy, haughty demeanor and yes, Starr still resented the old bat over a decade later.

"Like threatening to tell my mother would have made a difference to me. I wanted you and that's all that mattered." He shrugged with the easy attitude of a man who could have anything he wanted.

And he wanted her. The depth of that discovery made her forget to chew her toast for a full two seconds.

He wouldn't have cared what his mom thought? All these years she'd worried about his mother and he brushed aside her concerns with a simple sentence. Starr darn near went deaf for a moment as the notion settled and she faced the reality of her own insecurities and how she'd let Mrs. Hamilton-Reis play on them.

Starr shook herself free of the past and back into the moment. David was laying out some heavy stuff here and she didn't want to miss a word of it.

"Miss Sullivan told me I was hurting you by making you sneak around. That you had walked in the shadows and been ashamed too long. You deserved to be proud of who you are." He studied the handle on his coffee mug for an extended moment before taking a long swallow.

Aunt Libby's words had obviously bothered him.

It made total sense now. "That's why you asked me to go to the senior dance with you." It made total sense—and stung even now that he'd had to be pushed.

"No. I had already asked that."

Relief sluiced over her far stronger than she liked to admit. Something that had happened so long ago shouldn't have had this much power over her. But it did. *He* did.

"I'd already figured it was time to do the dating thing. We'd gotten things out of order because you made me so freaking hot I couldn't make it to dinner. I wish I could blame that impulsiveness on teenage hormones, but the hell of it is, I'm still as hot for you as I ever was."

Her skin heated all over at the admission. Did that make a second vulnerability he'd confessed? No. It didn't count when he knew full well she shared every bit of the impulsive, undeniable passion.

"We ditched our clothes pretty quickly around each other once you came back from that fancy boarding school of yours."

"You grew. God, did you ever grow up." His heated gaze scorched right over her, firing her up when her body should have been sated from their night of lovemaking. How could a woman with thighs that still ached be so totally entranced by a glance?

"As did you." She soaked up the hard-muscled look of him. Would she ever tire of simply seeing him? A scary notion because it scratched out the possibility of finding happiness anywhere else. "What did you do after Aunt Libby's big intimidating talk?"

"I asked you to come with me to college, to follow me around the world." He lifted a lock of her hair and teased it over the curve of her breast exposed by the gaping pajama top she wore, which made the satiny fabric feel all the more sexy against her skin because it was his. "I'm asking you again."

Why did he always have to try and distract her with sex? She only just now realized his every offer came with a sensual touch.

Starr met his gaze dead-on and tried her best to stifle the arousal zinging through her veins. "Nothing's changed, David."

"Sure it has. We're older. You can study the art you used to spend all those hours studying in pictures."

He really knew how to go for the jugular in a non-sexual way after all. She'd never been able to afford college, but had soaked up as much of art history as she could on her own. Still, growing up in a neighborhood of privilege, money, Ph.D. This and Dr. That, she couldn't help the occasional tweak to her self-esteem as she longed to go back to school.

Damn it, she'd made a successful business for herself and, while she made the arts and crafts for fun, her landscape paintings that she slid into the shop sold well.

David leaned closer in her silence, the heat of his body reaching to hers with a familiarity that never failed to stir her.

His mouth skimmed hers, his words heating her skin, as well as her desires. "We can make love in more exotic places than you can imagine."

She wanted. How could she not? His plan sounded enticing. But what about when she grew weary of travel and wanted to return home? She knew from David's in-frequent visits that their timetables for travel differed by quite a few months.

And what about permanence?

Uh-oh. She was thinking that *L* word. They'd said it all the time in high school. But didn't many teens toss the word around with the frequency of their fashion changes?

Still, she needed to be realistic. This man had held a place in her thoughts, in her world, for over half her life.

She would be a fool not to consider the possibility that she might just love the arrogant bastard. And if she loved him, then someday she might want the whole shebang.

Marriage. Oh, God.

Kids. Oh, God, oh, God.

Matching rocking chairs and grandchildren. Where was a paper bag because she was going to hyperventilate any second now.

This time together hadn't helped her at all. They'd only complicated things more by opening up all the old wounds from the past. She still wanted him and he was still as committed to his plan to live his life on the road. His whole romantic getaway was nothing more than an elaborate plan to entice her over to his way of thinking.

Wait. Rather than getting all bent out of shape, maybe it was time to show him she wasn't the same vulnerable teen he'd been with before. He wanted to show the benefits of his way of living.

Well, two could play that game.

Ten

Striding up the steps to his house, David planted his hand firmly in the small of Starr's back, reminding himself to be patient. He'd negotiated localized cease-fires between warring militants in hostile territories around the globe. Surely he could talk one woman into giving him a second chance. In the middle of their conversation over brunch, Starr had insisted she wanted to put their discussion on hold until they returned home, and simply enjoy the trip as he'd planned.

Once they'd returned to Charleston, she'd overheard his mother was at her weekly doctor visit. Starr had insisted she'd wanted a copy of their high-school prom photos. She'd said the copies at Aunt Libby's house had been damaged when the roof had leaked during a tropical storm. Did he have any left?

Sure. He thought there were some in a trunk in the attic.

Time alone was fine by him since he'd already managed to log a quick call to the local police department to check on queries into the Ciminos and debit-card fraud. The mall video footage was on its way to him for ID. Meanwhile, he took comfort in the fact that Starr seemed intent on giving her relatives a wide berth.

He closed the door behind him and turned to find Starr staring up at the cavernous hallway. She'd been in his house before, but not often. He tried to see the space through her eyes, but could only pull up his own feelings about the place with his mother's brittle brand of love— her lack of warmth rooted in murky memories David rarely allowed. Echoes of his father's temper filtered through his head against his will. The reverberation of the slammed front door as his father walked out time after time. His mother's stifled cries.

Darkness. That's all he saw here. Even with all the curtains opened, the house held an innate gloominess he couldn't find the imagination to dispel.

Starr pivoted on her heels. "This truly is a beautiful mansion."

He grunted, resting his hands on an antique brass Chinese lion head. The stuff childhood nightmares were made of.

"You don't agree?"

"It's smothering." He patted the lion on the head, moving on to the lion's mate.

"That's only because your mother insists on staying with the over-cluttered decor theme of heavy velvets and dark brocades."

He frowned, reevaluated. She had a point but he still couldn't imagine a simple coat of paint could chase away his father's gloomy taint. "What would you do?"

Starr swept her hands through the air. "Take all those curtains down and replace them with white shutters over there and whispery sheers there. Let the light shine through. Why live on the water if you're going to deny yourself the view?"

She hesitated, stopping at a line of posed studio photographs along the mantel and the oil portrait above. More stilted framed pictures lined the antique grand piano that no one played yet his mother insisted made a pivotal focal piece of furniture.

"Don't stop," he said nudging her, enjoying the sound of her voice more than the words per se. He wasn't convinced the house could be saved, but if anyone could revitalize the space, Starr could. "What else would you do?"

She tugged one of her ever-present hair scrunchies out of her pocket and pulled back her curls as if prepping herself for the task. "You probably won't like to hear this but I would ditch half the furniture and recover the rest in a lighter color, stripes I think, rather than those dark cabbage roses."

"Streamlining life." David nodded. She could start

with pitching the lions off the dock if it wouldn't give his mother a heart attack on the spot. "Why wouldn't I like that?"

She tapped a finger along a line of photos. "I can't imagine someone wanting to get rid of their heritage."

"Maybe I don't think of it that way because I've always had it."

Starr lingered on a photo of him with his parents when he'd been in first grade. "I wish I'd been able to get to know your father."

He grunted, not at all eager to linger on this topic of discussion. "Come on." He gestured toward the lengthy hall, Persian rug running the length. "The attic stairs are this way."

"It must have been difficult losing him so young. That put a lot of weight on you to be the man of the house as a teenager."

Obviously he hadn't warded off the topic as easily as he'd wanted. "I guess you could put it that way. But seriously, there's no need to make a sob story out of it. It's not like I had to quit school and support the family. He left us with a fat portfolio and an honest executor to look out for things until I was old enough to take over."

"When was old enough?"

"Twenty-one."

She hesitated at the base of the attic stairs. "You took over the books on this place when you weren't even done with college?"

"I let the executor hang on for about eighteen more

months." He passed her and yanked the dangling chain to turn on the attic light. Three bare bulbs lit the dusty A-frame nook beneath the roof, light from outside streaming in through a circular window at either end of the room. "Then I took the guy to court once he and I started disagreeing on some investments. I felt he was too conservative."

"Conservative can be good though."

He stared her up and down as she followed him on the narrow staircase to the attic. "I can't believe I'm hearing that from a woman in a pink fringed jacket and purple jeans."

"I happen to be very frugal when it comes to my finances." She sniffed.

"That's good. Very good in fact. But there's frugal, and there's sluggish." He extended a hand to help her maneuver the last step around into the attic. "At the rate he was going, there wouldn't be enough to keep my mother in the style to which she'd become accustomed. For myself, I don't give a flying f—uh, fig."

He made his way around trunks and enough dusty furniture to fill another house. Passing a family cradle his mother had bugged him more than once about filling, he stopped by the trunk he'd been seeking. "I support myself and the trust fund is just a bonus I was born into but am fully aware I didn't earn. But I will make sure my mother is cared for. That's my duty. My old man owes her after what he put her through."

Damn, he'd said too much. He reached for the lock

and jimmied it with the special tool he kept on his key chain, a nice perk of his job. He held the door and gestured her inside.

"What he put her through?" She plunked down onto an old wooden rocking horse. "What do you mean?"

"Nothing."

"You meant something or you wouldn't have said it." She toyed with the dusty yarn-mane on the horse's neck. "I thought we were past holding back from each other."

He still wondered how she'd ended up at Libby Sullivan's. He knew he could find the information in a snap by checking out the Ciminos, but he couldn't escape the need to have Starr tell him.

"I just meant the long hours he put in at the office." David kept his head ducked down and worked the trunk lock even though he'd jimmied it free first twist through. "All the parties and support she gave him as he climbed the corporate ladder."

"Bull."

"What?" Startled, he looked up from the lock.

"Bull. You're lying to me." Her hand stroked absently down the horse's mane even though she'd long ago swiped it free of dust. "You may be an amazing inter-rogator. But you're a crummy liar."

"I am not." He was the number-one agent in his office, damn it. He swung open the trunk lid with extra force. "I can lie my ass off quite well, thank you very much. Many a time my life has depended on my keeping a cover."

"Then it must be that you can't lie to me."

That said too much about the two of them and why they always ended up like this, two very different people, working like hell to resolve their differences and beating their stubborn heads against the wall.

He tugged out a stack of envelopes from the trunk and smacked them on the floor in front of her. How ironic to see labels with his mother's scrawl indicating memorabilia from his parents' dating days. He couldn't envision his autocratic father courting anyone.

David thumbed through other folders until he finally uncovered the one he'd labeled as theirs after the prom. He passed it to Starr. Her hands shaking ever so slightly, she took it from him, twisted open the metal tines and pulled out a stack of photos with reverent slowness.

One after the other, she took her time with the candid shots Libby Sullivan had taken of the two of them together in their prom finery. How like Starr to totally ignore the formal portrait shot altogether. And how like his family to have a houseful of formal portraits.

He reached to gather up the extra copies of the posed picture under a floral arch, both of them so young. Starr's hair had been longer—he could still remember the thrill of it wrapping around him during sex for the first time. The white dress she wore accented her dusky skin, her dark eyes and hair. It could have been a wedding dress. In those days he'd dreamed of seeing her wear one.

And of course he wore the standard tuxedo. Had he really owned his own tux at seventeen? His folks had made their plans for him known. Follow in the old man's footsteps... Except his father had just died, leaving David with a boatload of unresolved feelings about his home life.

He plopped the prom shots on top of the folders. It was time to stop pounding his head against the wall when it came to Starr. Thoughts of his father made him realize he didn't want to perpetuate the Reis brand of autocratic coldness in his own life. "My father was a cold bastard. His banking job, the almighty dollar, his clubs and golfing with powerful senators, that's all that mattered to him. My mother's family name was merely a means to that end. I was nothing more than the heir to carry on the legacy. His legacy. His name living on."

She rested her hands on her knees and leaned forward with earnest intensity. "Except you threw it in his face and went your own way."

"Yeah, I did." He met her nose to nose, no dodging her eyes, no shielding his expression from hers. "He had all the paperwork laid out for his alma mater and just expected I would do things his way. We never really talked about anything in our house. Things just 'happened.' Except this didn't happen. I told him no and explained my plan for my life."

"What happened?"

"He backhanded me. Then put the pen in my hand."

She gasped. Her mouth opened and closed once, then twice. He waited for the platitudes that would help him distance himself from her...then she simply laid her hand on top of his. Damn it. Her silence and simple touch, the way she looked right into his eye connected in a way far more intense than any words.

His throat moved in a swallow and a slow clearing. "As I held that pen with my face stinging, I could only think that was the first time my father had touched me in as long as I could remember."

Tears streaming down her face, Starr's arms went around his neck as she slid from his childhood rocking horse into his lap. "Oh, David, I'm so sorry."

She pressed her mouth to his before he had time to come up with some lam-ass excuse about how it didn't matter even though they both knew it really did. Of course it did. How could it not?

Her tears seared his skin clean through, more leaking and falling until they mingled with the taste of her on his lips.

He slid his arms around her, gathering her closer and soaking up the familiar feel and comfort of having her close, her hands stroking his face, shoulders, chest with gentle healing. Thank goodness she seemed to have sensed he'd had enough of deep discussion for now. Maybe communicating on a sexual level might be shallow, but the connection offered a hotter forgetfulness he needed so damned much.

Starr kept exerting pressure with her kiss and her body until he realized she'd leaned him backward onto the floor. The unforgiving hardness of the wood should have bothered him, but with soft and oh-so-giving Starr above him, he didn't give a crap where he lay so long as she kept on writhing on top of him. Stroking him, murmuring sweet words of affirmation and want.

"How much longer until your mother returns?"

"She's gone shopping. Two more hours at least."

"Thank goodness."

And just that fast, she'd undone his pants, and he wasn't slow on the uptake, so he worked her jeans down while she kicked them off.

Glory be, he did so love the easy access of a thong.

"Birth control. Condom."

She held out his wallet.

He frowned. "When did you get that?"

"I'm a pickpocket from way back. Remember? Apparently the touch stays with a person."

That shouldn't have made him laugh, but somehow it did. The incongruity of them always had messed with his mind. He flipped open his wallet, pulled out a condom and sheathed himself.

Breathless, he thunked his head. "Damn it. I'm worse than a fumbling horny teenager. You probably want a soft bed and foreplay and—"

Starr clapped a hand over his mouth. "I don't want foreplay this time. We'll do foreplay next time." She panted, staring down at him with heated intensity. "I want you. Hard. Fast. Now."

She emphasized the last word with a wriggle of her hips, nothing more than the scant scrap of damp lace of her thong separating them. But not for long.

He swept aside the skimpy barrier and slid inside her,

where he belonged. Her fingers fisted in his shirt, clawing at his skin through the fabric as the wriggle of her hips urged him on.

Sure, she could say no foreplay but he had to touch her. His hands itched for the feel of her. His fingers crawled up inside her shirt to cup her breasts. She moaned a plea and moved faster above him, their bodies inching along the floor with memorabilia from their past scattered around them, prom tickets and pictures.

The moist heat of her clenched around him until his head thunked back on the floor and he clenched his jaw with restraint. Tougher and tougher to hang on by the second and not made any easier by the sweet feel of her soft buttocks, but he couldn't bring himself to let go. Instead, he gripped her tighter, guiding her against him in grinding rhythm that had her gasping and moaning in time with his own pounding pulse.

Not much longer. He couldn't last much longer. But damned if he would finish before she did.

He slid a hand around between them, finding her tight bud, teasing her for…ah, her tongue peeked out between her teeth in her telltale sign that she was close, thank goodness. Then, she gasped and he forced his eyes to stay open while he waited and watched the seductive vision of her completion wash over her.

The second she collapsed on top of him, limp, replete, he cut the bonds and let go, the power of his own release tearing a shout from him he couldn't control.

But finally he admitted it to himself, he'd never been

in total control of his emotions around this woman. If he thought so, he'd only been lying to himself. All he could do was ride the wave until his heart slowed enough for him to hear the sounds around him again.

Starr breathing against his ear.

The creak of the wooden horse moving because apparently one of them had kicked it as they'd writhed on the floor.

An air-conditioner unit kicking on below stairs.

And as he gathered Starr closer to him, David realized he'd been lying to himself in more ways than one. He'd been certain he could make it all work, his grand plan for her to follow him around the world. With her in his arms, he realized he knew her. *Knew* the essence of this woman and traveling the world wasn't what she wanted.

So where did that leave him?

Where did that leave *them?*

Because for the first time he had to admit the truth to himself. He couldn't give her up.

"I give up." Starr flopped back in her chair, ceding control of the remote to her sister. "There's nothing decent on television this time of night."

"Why don't you go to bed then? I have to stay up with the baby till she nurses again." She tickled her wide-awake daughter's toes as little Libby grinned in the swing. "But that doesn't mean you have to miss out on sleep, too. Catch an extra hour for me."

Starr shook her head. "I'm too wired."

"From your trip or from work this evening?"

From making love in the attic, but she didn't feel like sharing that intensely intimate moment with her sister. As a matter of fact, a big part of the restlessness stemmed from feeling raw after all the sharing with David.

No wonder he was distant so much of the time. He'd had precious few examples of how to be affectionate. Only a smothering mother—who wanted any part of that—and an emotionally sterile father. For so long she'd demanded that he give her more of himself and he'd been offering her everything he had to give.

She swiped her hand under her nose and glued another ticket to the memory book, mounting it on a decorative movie-strip paper.

Claire reached across the kitchen table. "What's that you're working on? Something new for the gift shop?"

"No, this is for me. I'm making a memory book."

"It's about time you did one of those for yourself. The one you started for baby Libby is gorgeous. You have such a great eye for colors. I'm envious of how you put those together."

Starr snorted in disbelief. "You're so organized I would think you'd be great at these."

"Oh, I have my photos in boxes, filed by date, but when it comes to the cutting and the arranging, that's beyond me."

"I imagine we have skills that match up, which is

why we make good business partners." Starr sifted through the photos, searching for just the right one to center on the next page, finally settling on one of her and David sitting together in front of a bonfire. "I was talking to David about how Aunt Libby had a real gift for helping us find our strengths. God, I couldn't believe how lucky I was to have landed here."

The photo called to her to linger. She traced her finger over the two of them, so young, so long ago. David had his lanky arms looped around her as she grinned. Only now did she realize how few photos captured him smiling.

Claire's voice slowly pierced her reminiscent fog....

"I loved Aunt Libby, make no mistake about it. That dear woman mothered me from the time I was six. But in those early years, after I got past the aching for my own teenage mama—as unfit as she may have been—I yearned for a family. The fact that my own biological mother refused to sign away her parental rights was a mixed blessing. I never had abandonment issues, but I never could be set free, either. I was terrified of losing control of my environment. It took me long time—and a stubborn man—to share control with him and make this family of my own I wanted so desperately."

Where was Claire going with this? Claire always had a reason for her rambles, so Starr settled back and waited for the moral.

"When it came to abandonment, Ashley had it in

spades. Her birth parents didn't want the financial obligations of her birth defects." Her hand grazed over her
own infant's head as if to recheck the baby's health.
"And neither did adoptive parents. At least as a ward of
the state she had most everything fixed, God love our
precious little sister."

A little sister whose willowy stature towered over
both of her shorter older sisters now.

Starr couldn't help but think of her own trust issues
and imagine how much more difficult it would have
been had she been in Ashley's shoes. "It's going to be
hard for her to trust enough to fall in love."

Claire pierced her with a pointed stare, staying silent.

Starr fidgeted in her seat, suddenly uncomfortable
with all those pictures. She smacked the memory book
closed. "Now that you've covered your past and
Ashley's, I assume you want me to sort through my
own non-adoptive issues."

Still, her sister stayed diplomatically silent, lifting her
baby from the swing and settling her on her lap to nurse.
Did Claire realize how lucky she was to have found
such peace with her big hunk of a husband and the sweet
baby? Even thinking about that kind of normalcy felt un-
attainable, larger than life somehow, swelling frustrated
feelings inside Starr until she snapped.

"Fine." She shoved the memory book away. "Okay,
my family would have sold me for a piece of pizza and
that has left me with unresolved issues when it comes
to relationships."

And just that fast, stalwart Claire's smile faltered, her eyes welling until two tears spilled over down her cheeks. "That should tell you what complete and total idiots they are because you are the most amazing and unique individual I have ever met."

"Thank you." Starr's eyes started to sting, as well, and she reached across the table to clasp her sister's hand. "I love you, too. So what does all of this have to do with why I'm still single?"

"Think back, sweetie. Make a memory book in your mind and let yourself remember. Couples wanted to adopt you, regardless of your age. You were cute as could be, so dynamic, everyone *saw* you. You draw people in, always have." Her smile returned with a nose scrunch as she shook her head. "And yet, you always sabotaged it at the last minute by doing something awful to the couple to scare them away. Why do you think that was?"

Starr shoved her chair away and made tracks for the industrial-size refrigerator. Opening it, she searched. Where was a good hunk of chocolate when a girl needed it? "Well, it wasn't because I was holding out hope of going back to hawking encyclopedias door-to-door."

"Starr, I'm being serious here. This is important. Really important." Her voice chastised until Starr finally turned around with a slice of cheesecake in a napkin clasped in her hand.

Starr made her way back to the table and stuffed an

oversize bite in her mouth so she wouldn't have to answer the increasingly uncomfortable questions.

"You probably realize the truth of why you sabotaged everything, at least subconsciously, and that's why you're avoiding answering. You've been avoiding this for a long time."

Chewing, Starr let the words shuffle around in her head until they settled like the photos in her memory book, finding the right background and framing. And in a beautiful rightness, it all made sense. "I didn't want to leave David."

Claire sighed. "Of course you didn't."

Her sister made it sound so simple, yet it had taken ten years to work out. "I thought I was the bartender who dispensed wise advice."

"I've been subbing for you enough to get the gist of how it goes."

"You're damn good." Better than she'd given her credit for. Why hadn't she taken the time to listen before?

Because she hadn't been ready to listen.

Claire stroked a hand over her child's head and smiled indulgently at her younger sister. "Maybe I can sub at the bar for you while you're on your honeymoon."

Honeymoon? Panic twisted Starr's gut tighter than her fist working the last remnants from a tube of paint. Honeymoons came after a wedding. A wedding came after declarations of love.

Love. The word settled in her mind with the greatest sense of rightness of all, providing the perfect framework for all the snapshots of her and David together. How could she have looked at them in any other light? Of course she loved him—with everything inside her.

But thanks to her abandonment issues bred from a childhood of neglect, she'd been afraid this man who traveled the world would one day never return to her. Yet, he'd proved to her over the past ten years that even without her giving him the least encouragement, he'd stayed steadfast. He might be a hardheaded man, but he was *her* man, with issues of his own.

And even as a part of her started to make plans to claim him as her own, she couldn't help but stare out the window at the trio of RVs parked along the beach. Shame prickled over her. What did they want? A rogue thought she'd never considered swept over her as she allowed herself to consider a life with David for the first time.

If she surrendered to her feelings for David, would that put him in the Ciminos' crosshairs forever?

Eleven

Parked in the stifling library with his mother, David couldn't help but see the room through Starr's eyes, envisioning the room with light and—what had she said?—white shutters and sheers. She'd also wanted to clear the place of clutter.

That struck him most of all. Clear the clutter. His gaze stopped dead on the mantel and piano filled with photographs—stilted, posed portraits. Not to mention the mammoth posed oil portrait over the fireplace. Nowhere could he find the kind of laughter ever-present in snapshots taken by Libby Sullivan.

For probably the first time in his adult life, he let himself speak first without thinking. "Mother, why did you put up with Dad's crap for all those years?"

His mother froze, her teacup halfway to her mouth. Three blinks later, she placed her china cup back on the saucer with exaggerated care. "I'm not sure what you mean, dear."

He'd had enough of the denial. Sitting here in this stifling room, he couldn't help but wonder if he'd used his only-child status as an excuse to be a loner all these years. It was far easier than putting himself on the line in a conversation like this. It was certainly easier than risking getting his heart stomped by Starr.

Except now the danger of losing her outweighed anything else.

"You know exactly what I'm talking about." Something niggled in his brain right now, a reason why he needed to figure this out. "Mother, I deal with people telling falsehoods all the time in my job. It may not be the profession you would have chosen for me, but I'm damn good at it, good enough to wave the BS flag here. No disrespect meant, but you called me home. If you want something from me, the least you can do is be straight-up honest."

His mother turned the cup around and around on the saucer, a nervous twitch of hers. "Your father wasn't an overly demonstrative man. That simply wasn't his way. It doesn't mean he didn't love his family."

Enough already. "The only time he touched me was to pose for a photo or to backhand me. There's not much affection between us to build a relationship."

Lips pressed thin, she folded her hands in her lap.

"You never met your grandfather. Your father came a long way from how he was brought up."

"That might explain things, but it doesn't excuse them."

"Or why I didn't step in?"

He stayed silent. He hadn't been headed in that direction with this conversation, yet he couldn't bring himself to redirect the path.

"I did what I thought was right, son. I did what I thought would keep this kind of life for you. You have no idea what it's like to grow up with people looking down their nose at you because you don't have money."

His mother's family had all died before he was old enough to meet them. He'd known they didn't have much money, but she hadn't mentioned any great hardship. "If you know how it feels to be poor, why do you treat Starr and all the girls next door like pond scum?"

"Because I want you to keep the stature I've worked hard for you to gain." An edge of panic laced her tone. "I don't want your bloodline to backslide."

"Whoa, back this up." His brain went into overload with all the info she tossed his way in a few short sentences. "I thought you disapproved because some of the girls had rough pasts with illegal activities. Not because of some ridiculous bloodline issue that doesn't even matter."

"That's easy enough for you to say since you've never had to prove yourself."

Her spine straightened and she smoothed her hands over her completely wrinkle-free powder-blue dress.

He couldn't remember a time he'd seen his mother anything but perfectly groomed, gray-blond hair turned under at the chin.

All of the things spouting from his mother's mouth should have made her more sympathetic to the girls next door and instead she'd hardened her heart. Money versus bloodline? David didn't much like the new image of his mother forming in his mind. And he definitely didn't like the notion that this image was far from complete.

He shoved up from his seat, turning his back on his mother long enough to rein in his anger. "Starr is a part of my life." He cupped a family picture of the three of them and wondered what kind of family photo Starr would envision. They'd never even discussed children before. He hadn't given her much to hang her dreams on, a mistake on his part, one he could see now he needed to rectify.

Setting the framed picture facedown, David pivoted to face his mother. "Where she and I take the relationship next is up to her, but I will not push her away just because you don't approve of her DNA."

His mother shoved to her feet, quickly, with none of the frail shaking she'd displayed in the past few days. "Have you seen her parents? Her aunts and uncles and their schemes? What if they get a piece of that property? I've heard them talking, you know."

She made her way across the hardwood floor with a rapid *click, click, click* of her heels, her face flushed with anger rather than inflated blood pressure. "They want a share in that restaurant. They could be here permanently and then all our property values will drop. They don't care how they make it happen. These are the sort of people she comes from. Time will tell. *Blood* will tell. Just you wait and see."

"If it's the truth that blood will tell, then things do not bode well for me, Mother, given the way you've treated Starr."

She snapped. "How dare you."

Her rambling speech shuffled around in his head with niggling persistence, but he was close; his instincts insisted that if he continued to push, it would all make sense. "I dare much. I am your son, after all, your blood, Father's blood, and apparently I have your strength when it comes to standing by my decision. The difference is my decision isn't to protect a piece of property. I'm protecting a person. The only person who matters to me right now."

His mother raised a shaking hand and for a moment he actually thought she planned to hit him—until she pointed out the window. "Look at them. Look. You have to see. I thought that if you really looked at them…"

The truth hit him with far more power than any hand. His mother's sudden illness that had vanished. Her insistence he come home. The puzzle pieces fell into a picture he wished he didn't have to acknowledge. "You brought them here."

Her shaking stilled. His mother's arm lowered and she clasped her hands in front of herself in a white-knuckled clench. "I don't know what you're talking about."

"You called Starr's family here and then summoned me home. You set up this whole volatile meeting."

She tipped her chin. "So what if I did? There's nothing illegal in that. You've been mooning over that girl for more than ten years. It's kept you from finding a nice young woman to settle down with and give me grandchildren. What's wrong with an old woman wanting grandbabies to hold before she dies?"

"You're nowhere near death, Mother, but if you're that lonely, I believe the time has come for you to consider moving to an assisted-living facility. You have begun wandering and falling under the influence of people of bad repute. I can't watch over you 24/7."

Panic laced her blue eyes. "Then we will hire someone to move in here permanently."

"Someone you can sway over to your side and manipulate. I think you misunderstand. There's not a decision to be made."

"You're not asking me?" She blinked back the tears.

He couldn't allow her to stay here, not when she had this obvious wish to rain heartache on Starr's head. No matter what happened between him and Starr, he would protect her. "Mother, we can make this transition with grace and dignity, or we can do this in a way that hurts us both."

"You own the house. You're not leaving me any choice." She tipped her head with the regality of a deposed queen. All her tears disappeared in a snap.

He wasn't sending her into exile, for heaven's sake,

just someplace nearby with her friends where doctors and nurses could keep a better watch over her health.

"I won't send you far away to a hovel. You are my mother and you will see me just as often as you do now. But I will not allow you to hurt Starr." He closed the six feet between them and rested a hand on her shoulder. "And Mother, I will not allow you to hurt yourself through a vendetta that eats you alive."

"I'm not a bad person. I didn't do such a terrible job bringing you up, after all."

"That's neither here nor there. So we have come to an agreement?" He gave her shoulder a gentle squeeze before stepping back. "One thing boggles my mind though, Mother. Why go to all this trouble? Starr and I resolved long ago we're not right for each other—for reasons totally different than yours of course. Why try to break us up when we aren't a couple?"

"Oh, my son, are you truly that self-unaware?"

He stared, unblinking.

"You've been obsessed with this girl since she pulled up in the driveway seventeen years ago, long before you even started dating. I don't know what kind of hold she has over you. Maybe it has something to with how these people are able to pull off such unbelievable scams—"

"Mother…" he growled.

She waved a hand in the air. "Whatever. The two of you play at this game and it doesn't seem to make you happy. I only want my son to be happy."

"Do you think being manipulated by my mother

makes me happy? Do you think being mortified by her family has made Starr happy?" He thought of her tears in the attic, her tears for him. He'd been a fool for leaving her behind all these years. She deserved better than she'd gotten from the people in his house. "I stand by my statement. Life moves on and it's time for us to make some adjustments. If you truly want those grandchildren, there's only one woman who will be their mom."

He'd made his point and she could accept it or not, he wasn't backing down. But since he'd won his point, he felt compelled to let her know something he'd perhaps forgotten to say often enough. He leaned to kiss her cheek. "I do love you."

"Thank you, son." She backed away toward the hall. "I believe I'll go call Bitsy from my old bridge club. I hear she's happy with the retirement home...."

Her voice faded as she made her way to the stairs.

Well, hell. She hadn't even bothered to say she loved him back. His parents really were a mess in the emotional department. No wonder he was so screwed up when it came to giving Starr what she needed.

What she deserved after being so horribly used by that clan of hers.

Except after her years with Aunt Libby, perhaps Starr had some things she could teach him in the emotional arena in exchange for the things he'd taught her in the bedroom.

What a sweet deal, now that he thought of it. It wasn't as if he were expected to be freaking Shakespeare shouting over a megaphone. These sorts of things were private. Awesomely private.

The time had come for him to accept the truth. He would take Starr any way he could have her, even if it meant curbing his travel.

Now that he'd made the decision, he didn't want to wait another minute in laying claim to his woman for life, and he knew just the thing to romance her artist's eye. Mind set, David reached for the family portrait over the fireplace, pulled it back to reveal a small safe and punched in the code. Making her happy would make him happy. She deserved that and more. He opened the creaking safe door to a small fortune.

He loved Starr. Always had, he just hadn't recognized the feeling since he'd had precious little example to compare it to at home.

But no more living in the dark, thanks to Starr. She'd thrown wide the windows to let in the light and he intended to do his best to persuade her they should spend the rest of their lives standing in the sunshine. Together.

But first, he needed to clear the beach of the traveler caravan, once and for all.

Starr juggled everything in her hands, wondering why she'd tried to carry so much at once. But then that was pretty much the story of her life. She always tried to take on too much, her eyes bigger than her stomach.

A big dreamer. Today, though, she hoped she could make all those hopes come true.

Under one arm, she carried a memory book she'd made, but it wasn't of she and David. In the stack of folders, she'd found an extra accidentally included one containing family photos of David as a baby. The photos of David's father were sweet, as well, the proud papa, a happy husband. Things may have gone bad in the Hamilton-Reis household later on, but at one time, they'd been better.

Starr couldn't help but think of how she'd been dating David as his mother had been grieving the loss of her husband. That couldn't have been easy. And in that little revelation, Starr was able to ease up on some of her anger. She might not like the idea of a clingy mother hanging on to her son, but at least she could understand on some level.

Under her other arm, she held the cat plate. She'd bought a reproduction for herself, doggone him and his gold credit cards. And finally, she held a cat carrier with an orange tabby inside.

For the first time, she trudged up the steps of David's house by herself.

She rang the bell and waited and waited. Nothing happened. She started to turn away—

Behind her, the front door creaked open. She spun around to find David's mother standing there, and surprise, surprise, the older woman looked rather rumpled, bringing to mind her front-porch visit of just a week ago. As much as Starr resented the way she'd been treated over the years, she had to get along with this woman. At least David would know Starr had tried.

Starr thrust the kitty carrier toward her. "I remembered you used to have a cat back when I first moved in. This one isn't all fluffy like the Persian cat you used to have, but pound pets are usually really grateful for the love. And it matches this amazing collector's item plate."

"Um, my dear, I'm not sure what to say." Alice Hamilton-Reis looked around her for others, no little surprise on her face.

"It's probably best you don't say anything. I just wanted to bring you a get-well gift since you've been feeling under the weather." Starr passed the album and took a deep breath since things were going to get a bit stickier now. "David gave me these photos to organize into this gift for you."

"*David* gave it to you?"

The pathetic hopefulness in her voice softened up a hard spot in Starr's heart. She figured David would forgive her the slight fudge with the truth.

"Yes, ma'am. You know that David and I have been friends—and more—for a long time now. He means a lot to me, which makes you a special person in my life, too. I hope that you will accept this memory album as a peace offering, a fresh start for a new relationship between you and I—for David's sake if nothing else."

The older woman took the album, staring at the wedding photo of herself with David's father. Mrs. Hamilton-Reis had clearly loved the man. Maybe the loss of that love had simply devastated her so deeply she didn't have much to offer anyone else.

Alice Hamilton-Reis's fingers shook as she traced the posed picture. "This is truly lovely, the way you've matted the portrait. Thank you." She smiled, albeit begrudgingly. "You have a good eye for mixing colors. I've always liked the flower bed you planted around the carriage house."

The woman obviously still adored her prize tea roses, but it was nice to hear she could see the beauty of a rambling cottage garden, too. Starr set down the cat and plate with hope in her heart.

A shriek sounded in the distance.

She pivoted, searched, finally peered around the corner of the house to find… Her relatives were all outside their campers, clustered around David—and a pair of police officers. Ohmigod. How had she missed that as she'd walked across the lawn? Likely because she'd done her best to keep her eyes averted from the problem.

Now she couldn't take her eyes off it. "Here, Mrs. Hamilton-Reis. You don't have to decide now about the cat. Just think it over. If you don't want the cat, I'll take it, but I really hope you'll enjoy her."

She'd read a lot about how much a pet could do to help alleviate depression in someone battling loneliness.

Starr charged down the steps toward the fray. "David? David! What's going on?"

Her petite mother ran to her, arms extended, flitting like a bird. "Oh, sugar, thank goodness you're here. You can straighten all this out before suppertime. Your boyfriend here thinks we're criminals. You know we would never hurt anyone."

Other than leaving a kid to suffocate in an RV. Or ripping people off with crap items. Or stealing from an old woman who took in cast-off children. Starr suffered through the hug before crossing to David. "What's the matter?"

He peeled her mother's hands off Starr's arm. "The police have questions about a series of debit-card scams in Dallas. They believe your family is responsible."

She didn't doubt for a second the Ciminos en masse could pull something like that off.

Frederick clapped a hand on David's back. "Young man, surely you can use some of your connections to help us out here."

David shook his head. "Actually, my connections are the ones who tracked this down and reported it."

Starr gasped. Gita grabbed her daughter's hand again like a last-minute lifeline. Starr had to look in her mother's eyes and deny the connection that had only hurt her. At least Mrs. Hamilton-Reis—in her own halting way—had admitted when she'd been wrong. Whereas Gita was still incapable of admitting she'd made mistakes. Starr turned to David and realized he was worried about her reaction.

His gaze met and held hers as if gauging her feelings. Did he really think she would be angry? Great gracious, she'd been waiting all her life for someone to help her take them on. Aunt Libby had tried, but she'd had so many children with problem families, there hadn't been much of her to spread around.

Heavens, she wasn't in the least angry. She hooked a hand in the crook of David's arm, physically choosing him over the parents who'd only hurt her. "I appreciate David's help. We don't want anything questionable going on around Beachcombers." She lowered her voice, but added a wealth of steel. "You lost me the day you left me to roast in the RV for hours on end until the cops finally discovered me and took me to a hospital. I almost died, you know. But I won't regret it, though, since your criminal carelessness brought me here."

She needed to vocalize her stance to ensure all the Ciminos knew where she stood, even as she felt the flex of muscles in David's arm under her touch at the mention of her parents' neglect. Essie scrambled away first, realizing the jig was up.

Gita and Frederick backed away more slowly, eyes and noses narrowed. Undoubtedly they would get away with community service hours. They were slippery that way. But they were also savvy enough never to pull a scam again in a town where the cops caught their scent.

Such as Charleston.

Relief flowed through Starr's veins as old worries slid from her shoulders. David had accomplished so much more than banishing her relatives from her land. He'd helped her see what she really wanted from her life. For the first time, she was brave enough to dream about a future that included love. Laughter.

Starr squeezed David's elbow again as she watched

her relatives load up in the Cimino gypsy caravan for what she felt certain was the last time she would ever see them. He looped an arm around her shoulders as the cop cruiser escorted the rickety vehicles onto the main road.

She tipped her face up to his, smiling. "Thank you."

"You're more than welcome. I'm sorry it took me so long to get it right, but I swear they will never hurt you again. I just wish I could have been there to help you when you were a defenseless ten-year-old locked in that damn camper." His embrace grew so tight it bordered on painful.

She hugged him back, realizing right now the event hurt him more than it did her. "It's okay, David. *I'm* okay. It's in the past and thanks to you, they are in my past."

"Damn straight," he rasped, his voice more than a little raw.

He started to lean down to kiss her when a screech split the air. He jerked upright. "What the hell is that?"

She fidgeted, embarrassed and grinning and so in love all at once. "Uh, I believe that's your mother's cat."

"My mother's cat?"

They both turned and, sure enough, there stood David's mother on the side veranda observing the whole ordeal—tabby cat in her arms, tucked under her chin. Alice showed that animal more affection than Starr had seen her give any human, but at least the woman was smiling for a change.

It was a start.

David tucked Starr closer to his side. "I assume it's

no coincidence that animal resembles the one in the gallery plate."

"You're an observant man. I thought she could use some companionship."

"I would kiss you senseless right now for being so thoughtful in spite of everything, but my mother's watching so that would be rather weird." He skimmed her hair away from her face. "Although that's a temporary situation. She and I had a discussion this afternoon about her going to a retirement village."

Shock rooted Starr to the spot. She couldn't have heard him right…. But searching his eyes, she saw that she had. There was more to this than he was saying, but regardless, she sensed that he'd done this for her. And from the way his mother held the cat that had come from Starr, maybe there was hope for all of them after all.

Starr settled deeper into David's embrace. "Well, from the look of things, I imagine you'd best make sure they take cats at the place."

"Money's no object, remember?"

"Of course, Agent Money Bags." She arched up to brush a quick, quite circumspect kiss across his lips. "Although if we're going to keep things low-key with your mother around, you should probably stay right here for a while until your body calms down."

"Those are just the family jewels in my pocket." He hugged her tighter with a secretive smile on his face. "Meet me on the pier at midnight and I'll let you check them out."

* * *

Music from Beachcombers drifted on the ocean breeze. Starr owed Ashley big time since she was closing the bar for her tonight. But her romantic younger sister had been more than happy to help her out. It felt strange to openly acknowledge the possibility of a relationship with David, but the time had come for them both to step into the light.

Speaking of which, he stood at the end of his family's dock, a lone bulb streaming light down over him. After all these years, he still stole the air from her lungs. Tall and dark and lean. As a scared, neglected gypsy child, she hadn't believed she deserved someone like him.

Now, thanks to his steadfastness, she knew she totally deserved his love.

"David."

He leaned back against the wooden railing. "Starr."

Just the simple speaking of their names carried a wealth of emotion. He extended a hand. She linked her fingers with his and stepped into his embrace.

For countless laps of the waves against the moorings, she stood in the warmth of his arms, enjoying the wealth of colors in the moonbeams streaking across the deep purple water.

She nestled her head under his chin. "What's this about family jewels?"

His laughter rumbled against her back. "I'll get to that in a minute. I have a few things I want to tell you first, things I should have figured out a long time ago." She felt his neck work in a long swallow. "I'm willing to cut back on the travel so you can have the home you need. You need those roots and I'm damn sorry I didn't see that before. The house is ours for you to bring light inside."

She squeezed her eyes tight against the tears threatening to pop free. She'd waited so long for this. She rubbed his hands over her stomach. "I'm not averse to taking a few road trips with you now and again. I think I would like to get an art degree and seeing the artists' work for real would only help my studies."

"I think that's an incredible idea. I've learned to see my home through new eyes because of you. Hell, I've learned to see life through new eyes because of you. Home has a definite new allure with you in it. And you'll be next door to Beachcombers whenever work calls."

She stared down at their clasped hands and let words slip free she hadn't dared share with anyone before, but then she'd never had David in her life for good before. "I have to confess to being a little jealous of Ashley when she graduated."

"Yet you still gave her the degree first." He turned her to face him and cupped the back of her head. "You're a helluva woman."

"She needed it more." The choice had been clear if not easy.

"Like I said, helluva woman. Is it any wonder I love you?"

"You love me?" She'd thought so, hoped so, but hearing him voice it meant more than she could have even imagined.

"Of course I love you. I asked you to marry me, didn't I?"

"Uh, no. You didn't. I would have remembered that."

"Damn, I'm messing this all up."

She rather liked jumbling the brain of this normally suave man, although it wouldn't hurt to give him some encouragement. "Feel free to try again, because I love you so very much this is something I definitely want to hear."

"You love me, too, huh?" Grinning, he dipped his hand into his suit coat pocket and pulled out a green velvet bag. "Hold out your hands."

She cupped her fingers and he poured out a hefty assortment of jewels—two necklaces, a bracelet and three rings with emeralds, diamonds and sapphires. "Uh, wow?"

He laughed that wicked way of his. "Family jewels, remember?"

She threw back her head, joining in his laughter that tickled up her spine and always would. "And to think I had another sort of family jewels in mind."

David pressed a kiss to the side of her head. "You do make me smile, babe, and we'll get to those later if you're still of the same mind." He grazed down over her mouth, lingered for a sweep that had her toes curling in her flip-flops before he continued, "Seriously, these are just some of the heirlooms slated for my wife. I thought about the way you said you would redecorate the house and it occurred to me that you might have an idea for resetting some of these stones into an engagement ring. A one-of-a-kind look for the unique woman who stole my heart."

"Oh. Really wow. And holy cow, yes. Yes to your love and yes to making an engagement ring that show-cases our very unique love." She looked down at the jewels in her hands and tears stung her eyes. He really was trying to meet her halfway, seeing who she was and accepting their differences. And it was working.

A sigh of relief racked through him before he smiled down at her again. "Thank you for those generous gifts you brought over for my mother. I'm not so sure she deserved them, but the way you compromised means a helluva lot to me."

"She brought you up." She stared into his deep blue eyes so full of love for her she knew she would never mistake it again. "That's gift enough for me."

"Like I said, you're generous. And about that cat plate, you bought it for yourself."

"I have my own money, buster." She slugged him in his muscle-hard arm. "You seem to have forgotten that along the line somewhere."

He locked those steely arms around her, where she knew they would stay forever. "Before we see it coming, you'll be the millionaire in our relationship."

"Bet on it." She savored his confidence in her.

He dropped kisses onto her face, along her jaw, accenting every word with the taste of his passion. "Either way, I'm totally and completely under the influence of your charms."

* * * * *

*Here's a sneak peek of
Catherine Mann's next release.
Don't miss ON TARGET,
available this July from HQN Books.*

Over the Caribbean Sea: Present Day

"Blackbird 33, Blackbird 33, this is sentry 20 reporting a pirate ship ahead at your ten o'clock, twenty-eight miles."

Pirate ship?

The improbable sentry radio call rattled around in flight engineer Shane "Vegas" O'Riley's headset as he manned his station of the CV-22 aircraft. He couldn't have heard what he thought.

Sure they were over the wild and woolly Caribbean, but someone must be screwing with them. Air Force crewdogs were well-known for their practical jokes.

Except today, he couldn't be less in the mood for gags. This flight to deliver supplies served a dual purpose for him. He would also be making a stop at a tiny godforsaken island where his wife worked teaching in the latest needy village to cross her aid group's radar.

There, he would also deliver divorce papers to sign.

But back to these freaking pirates. Since the weather was dog crap, he was in charge of the radio while the two pilots had their hands full of bouncing airplane.

Shane thumbed the radio transmit key, sweat burning his eyes, his flight suit sticking to his back in the unrelenting summer heat. No AC could keep up. "Sentry did you say a pirate ship" Is Johnny Depp onboard with his swashbuckling costume? Do you want us to land this puppy on the poop deck and get his autograph for you?" Since the CV-22 took off and landed like a helicopter, then rotated the blades forward to fly like a plane, they actually could manage just such a feat if there was a pirate ship. "I'll tell him it's for your daughter if you're embarrassed."

The jerking craft jarred his teeth, hard, faster than the roller-coaster ride he'd taken with his two daughters at Six Flags last summer.

In front of him sat the two pilots. Aircraft commander Postal gripped the wobbling stick while newbie copilot Rodeo took wildly fluctuating system reads off the control panel. Shane glanced over his shoulder back into the belly of the craft to check on the three gunners—and yeah, thank God—they'd strapped their butts down tight.

Their radio crackled in the inclement weather, words sputtering through unevenly, "Pirates…guns at…cruise ship."

Some theme cruise perhaps? A pocket of turbulence whacked Shane's helmet against the overhead panel and rattled his brain worse than a baseball bat upside the temple. "I'm so not in the mood for this 'Argh' and 'Shiver me timbers' garbage. We've got a weather emergency here."

"Sorry," the radio voice claiming to be Sentry 20 responded, "not yanking you chain, Blackbird 33. We have a message relay from Southern Command Headquarters. Ready to copy?"

Shane straightened in his seat. "Really? No joke?" he said, still only half believing. "We'll play along for the heck of it, ready to copy."

The radio crackled to life. "Blackbird 33, proceed to one-eight dash zero-five north, zero-six-three dash five-nine west to intercept a pirate vessel, suspect to be terrorists, threatening a passenger cruise ship. We are ordered to disable the pirate boat—" the connection went staticy for another two jostles "—or destroy the pirate's vessel, a cigarette boat, if you or the cruise ship is fired on. Copy?"

An order to shoot a cigarette boat that just happened to be tooling around in the Caribbean Sea? This could be the worst kind of setup for an ambush in this lawless corner of the ocean. Unease prickled up Shane's spine as he could already envision his crewmember's faces plastered across the six o'clock news—and not in a good kind of way.

That would be a helluva way to end a career and a marriage in one fell swoop. "Who is this?"

"Listen up, Blackbird," the voice barked back, "I authenticated the communication when I got it and I think you should do the same."

Well, they got that right. "Rodeo, dig out the code book."

"Way ahead of you, Vegas. Here ya go." The copilot's normally easygoing demeanor was nowhere to be found as he passed back the book before quickly returning to the controls. Rodeo had his hands full running both his copilot's position and checking Shane's flight engineer regular duties monitoring engine and aircraft health since he had to deal with this buccaneer BS.

Vegas thumbed through the pages until he found what he needed. "Sentry, authenticate foxtrot-mike."

"Sentry, authenticates with zulu-tango."

"So, Sarge?" Rodeo's voice shot over the radio. "Is that correct?"

Holy crap. Shane verified it once, reread again. No movie-star autographs in their future today. This was the real deal. "That is the correct response, sir."

The aircraft commander, Postal, cursed into the interphone. "Well, spank my ass and get me an eye patch." Clicking over to radio to broadcast beyond the plane. "Good authentication, Sentry, we headed that way…. Rodeo, give me a—"

"Already on it," the copilot interrupted. He might be new to the craft but the man was a freaking genius, a quick thinker on his feet to boot. That worked well with a gut-instinct player like Postal. "Come left to heading one-seven-seven. Showing time to intercept at

CATHERINE MANN 177

eight minutes. Target is now twenty-seven miles ahead."

"Copy all." Postal's normally wired facade faded at the very real threat ahead—a flipping terrorist pirate ship, no less. "Crew, lock and load, cleared to fire a burst. Let's make sure those babies are working in case we need them."

Brrrrrp. Brrrrrp. The sound of quick bursts from electrically powered miniguns came through the helmets and the smell of gunpowder drifted up to linger in the cockpit. The right gunner, left gunner—Stones, Padre and Sandman—all checked in ready to go.

Both pilots looked out toward the horizon, searching for a sign of the boat. Shane kept his eyes forward, his thumb on the radio and tried not to think about the divorce papers in his flight bag. There wasn't much to divvy up. With Sherry living much of her life in one NGO tent after another. Most of her gear consisted of easy-to-pack toys for the kids.

His little girls, yet not legally his daughters. They were Sherry's, adopted during her first marriage—Cara from Vietnam and Malaika from the Sudan. And once the divorce went through, he would lose all rights to them. Ah, hell. His throat clogged. He'd just wanted to settle down, have a real family life. Sherry insisted she was living a real life around the world and he was welcome to join them anytime.

Where the hell was the compromise in that?

The aircraft commander cranked the craft in a flawless bank that pulled Shane to the dangerous present. Postal's wild eyes stuck to the horizon, his hand on the stick. "Work that radar hard, Rodeo. Let me know when you've got a bead on him."

"Roger that, start a right turn, shallow bank. Roll out. Straight ahead five miles."

The air grew heavier. Some might say with humidity, but Shane had been around, fought in enough conflicts to know that the minutes leading up to battle sucked emotions out of a person and pumped them into the air where they couldn't distract a man. Inside, he could stay emotionless. Eighteen years he'd served, since he'd given up a chance at a pro baseball career to enlist and go overseas to fight in the first Gulf War.

He'd never regretted the decision. But both careers spoke to the core of who he was, a good old-fashioned picket fence, baseball, flag waving and apple pie family man. He'd thought he'd found that with Sherry and the girls. He wanted to be the big strong dude who built a home for his family and protected them.

And by protecting, he'd meant from burglars. Not freaking pirate ships and tribal warlords that attacked tent villages. What the hell was she thinking hauling the kids around to unruly corners of the world like this?

Postal leaned forward, the air getting a good pound or two heavier until he said, "Okay, I got 'em visual. Start a turn to go around them. It's a cigarette boat. Get the infrared cam on them and see what they look like."

Rodeo nodded, sweat glistening on his bronze skin.

"Got a lock. Zooming cameras for confirmation…and ah, hell, big guns on that boat. I would say the pirates."

Pirate Captain Jack Sparrow didn't have a speed-boat like that.

The infrared screen display bloomed upward. Gun-fire from the boat. Aimed at the CV-22. No more questioning how to respond.

Heaven help them. This was it. Open combat to the death.

* * * * *

Turn the page for a sneak preview of
IF I'D NEVER KNOWN YOUR LOVE
by
Georgia Bockoven

From the brand-new series
Harlequin Everlasting Love
Every great love has a story to tell. ™

One year, five months and four days missing

There's no way for you to know this, Evan, but I haven't written to you for a few months. Actually, it's been almost a year. I had a hard time picking up a pen once more after we paid the second ransom and then received a letter saying it wasn't enough. I was so sure you were coming home that I took the kids along to Bogotá so they could fly home with you and me, something I swore I'd never do. I've fallen in love with Colombia and the people who've opened their hearts to me. But fear is a constant companion when I'm there. I won't ever expose our children to that kind of danger again.

I'm at a loss over what to do anymore, Evan. I've begged and pleaded and thrown temper tantrums with every official I can corner both here and at home. They've been incredibly tolerant and understanding, but in the end as ineffectual as the rest of us.

I try to imagine what your life is like now, what you do every day, what you're wearing, what you eat. I want to believe that the people who have you are misguided yet kind, that they treat you well. It's how I survive day to day. To think of you being mistreated hurts too much. If I picture you locked away somewhere and suffering, a weight descends on me that makes it almost impossible to get out of bed in the morning.

Your captors surely know you by now. They have to recognize what a good man you are. I imagine you working with their children, telling them that you have children, too, showing them the pictures you carry in your wallet. Can't the men who have you understand how much your children miss you? How can it not matter to them?

How can they keep you away from us all this time? Over and over, we've done what they asked. Are they oblivious to the depth of their cruelty? What kind of people are they that they don't care?

I used to keep a calendar beside our bed next to the peach rose you picked for me before you left. Every night I marked another day, counting how many you'd been gone. I don't do that any longer. I don't want to be reminded of all the days we'll never get back.

When I can't sleep at night, I tell you about my day. I imagine you hearing me and smiling over the details that make up my life now. I never tell you how defeated I feel at moments or how hard I work to hide it from everyone for fear they will see it as a reason to stop believing you are coming home to us.

And I couldn't tell you about the lump I found in my breast and how difficult it was going through all the tests without you here to lean on. The lump was benign—the process reaching that diagnosis utterly terrifying. I couldn't stop thinking about what would happen to Shelly and Jason if something happened to me.

We need you to come home.

I'm worn down with missing you.

I'm going to read this tomorrow and will probably tear it up or burn it in the fireplace. I don't want you to get the idea I ever doubted what I was doing to free you or thought the work a burden. I would gladly spend the rest of my life at it, even if, in the end, we only had one day together.

You are my life, Evan.

I will love you forever.

* * * * *